T0129323

The LOSS of an IDENTITY

Mary Ableman

authorHOUSE®

AuthorHouse™
1663 Liberty Drive
Bloomington, IN 47403
www.authorhouse.com
Phone: 1 (800) 839-8640

Published by AuthorHouse 02/25/2020

ISBN: 978-1-5462-4563-6 (sc)
ISBN: 978-1-5462-4562-9 (e)

Library of Congress Control Number: 2018906625

Print information available on the last page.

This book is printed on acid-free paper.

Contents

Prologue

It was a beautiful day in Cape Cod. Butterflies decorated the sky with their epoch beauty while the sun shone brightly all over his lawn, allowing him to forget the cold harsh winter that had passed as the first warm day of spring arrived. Winter usually didn't bother him. The snowfalls always seemed to pass quickly and when the occasional one came, it brought with it serenity and excitement, presenting a chance for children to build snowmen, make snow angels, and go sledding. It was also a reminder of those mornings when his children replaced the monotony in the routine of getting ready for school with the hopeful excitement of possibly having one of those magical snow days. This had been an unusual winter though; with frigid cold temperatures and snow that seemed to never stop falling from a colorless drab sky.

Typically, today would have been a tremendous day. The type of day he would dream about on those days when ice and snow found its way through heavy clothing, chilling his bones and soaking his socks regardless of his waterproof footwear. Aside from being cold and uncomfortable, these types of winters always left him in a constant panic of catching one of those winter colds that never seem to go away. He wasn't the type of man who had the luxury of being off his game, and taking a sick day was just unfortunately an impossibility. Missing work would mean missing a day in court and since he was always in the middle of some sort of high profile or important case that would mean putting others lives on hold. And that simply would not be ok. As judge, he was the one who oversaw an individual's fate, and the fate of all those connected to that individual. His role in helping to determine whether or not a guilty person went free or an innocent person rotted in jail was a responsibility that plagued him daily. His wife sometimes wondered why he chose his profession. But in his heart, he never saw it as a choice but as an unavoidable calling and though he regularly tried to explain it to his wife the reasons he was able to share did not paint the full picture.

The reason was clear every time he saw the face of a mother who just lost her son watch the killer get found guilty and go to jail; or every time he watched a victim take back a small piece of her life by confronting her rapist and seeing him get convicted; or even when he watched an innocent man accused of a crime being able to put the nightmare of court behind him when he was sent free to put his life back together. To his wife, however, he simply explained that he choose to do this because he wanted to be the protector of the innocent and most importantly, he wanted to make sure that his daughters lived in a world that was safe.

As these thoughts and memories streamed through his mind it almost seemed ironic to him, he should not be thinking about work he should simply be enjoying the beautiful day. This was the day that he had yearned for throughout that awful winter. This normally was the day that his mind was only filled with peaceful thoughts of nice weather and chirping birds. Right now though, one thought kept going through his mind. How did his most treasured day turn out to be the day that his world had crashed down upon him? How could God be that cruel to him? His professional life was perfect. His days in court had been very successful. But none of that mattered right now. It felt like none of that would ever matter again.

Today was the worst day a man could possibly imagine. It was a day he would never forget. Today he found out that all of his work was pointless. That everything he had worked for did not matter a damn. In his eyes he had accomplished absolutely nothing. Today a man's greatest fear had come true: one daughter dead and the other damned to live out the rest of her life not remembering her own identity.

***

I felt myself begin to slip out of a deep sleep due to the song of some very noisy birds. While some people would be annoyed by the intrusion into their sleep, I felt a content smile arise onto my lips as my awakening body was bathed in the sunlight that cascaded through the window above my bed. It felt like it had to be in the mid sixties. A perfect temperature to get my day started. As quickly as the smile appeared on my lips and the thoughts of the warm sun entered my mind the smile on my previously blissful face turned to a frown and the thoughts of the warm sun was replaced by the intense pain that seemed to be radiating throughout my entire body and mostly in my head.

I heard a surprisingly loud groan escape from my mouth as I opened my heavy eyelids confused at the pain. My uncertainty deepened when I glanced around the room to realize I had no idea where I was. I felt the panic build up inside my chest as I became familiar with my surroundings. It was an awful bright white room and I was surrounded by a variety of different flower arrangements. It appeared I was in some sort of hospital room. I continued to look round the room when a strange woman who looked to be in her late forties suddenly captured my attention. She sat next to me with a peculiar expression on her face. It was evident that she was worried due to the wrinkles that appeared across her forehead but there was more to her expression then just petty concern. Her mascara, which had once been applied quite heavily, was now smeared on her face making it very obvious she had been crying.

While my main focus was on my excruciating pain, my heart went out to her. There was an intense sadness that reflected out of her crystal blue eyes. It was strange that such a beautiful put-together woman could look so broken. She had a tragic look, like something you would see out of a soap opera, a mix of devastation and guilt. As these thoughts entered my mind she became aware that I was awake and focused on her. In a split second her vulnerability was replaced by the look of a woman ready to take action. She must have felt exposed in her moment of melancholy. "Chloe thank God you are awake!" she exclaimed.

"Chloe? Who is Chloe?" I managed to whisper in a soft voice, trying to ignore the agony that coursed through my entire body. "Why am I in a hospital? What happened to me? Oh screw it," I mumbled. "I just hurt, my head and body hurt so badly," I said, giving into the pain and confusion.

The woman's eyes flickered with sadness, shock and surprisingly even the slightest look of anger. "They told me there was a chance you wouldn't remember."

"Who? Who said that I wouldn't remember? Remember what?"

On cue, three men appeared in the room: one a middle age plump guy in a white doctor's coat; one an older distinguished looking man who was covered in a variety of bandages and another who was devastatingly handsome and appeared to be in his mid twenties.

All three of the men's eyes lit up when they saw that my eyes were open. "You're awake!" said the older man as if he was stating something profound to the group.

"How is my patient doing today?" asked the doctor in an annoyingly cheerful voice that for some reason just did not seem appropriate at the moment. "It's a good sign to see you awake and alert," he said as he walked over to me and looked in my eyes with a painfully bright light and spent time studying my pupils. "You woke up once before, but you were so out of it I doubt you even remember. So how do you feel?"

"She doesn't even know her own damn name! And she's in pain," cried the middle-aged woman in a livid voice before I could get my mouth open to respond.

The doctor did not seem phased by this but the other two men's eyes opened wide in shock. "Baby you have to remember your own name. You're just confused, tell them, tell them that you remember" said the attractive younger man in a soft voice as he walked over to the bed and grabbed my hand in his. The man looked me in the eyes and I don't know what my eyes showed him but his were filled with an intense fear.

Instantaneously I felt my eyes starting to fill with tears. I had no idea who these people were and I was in so much pain I could hardly bear it. I knew that if I could get the throbbing under control then I just might be able to sort everything else out.

"Ok, let's not overwhelm her too much," said the doctor as if he were instructing small children to behave. It was strange to have everyone stare at me with such hope. It was as if they were looking at me to tell them everything would be ok. They looked as if their worlds had just shattered and somehow I had the glue to piece them back together. The whole thing was surreal and peculiar to me since whatever my world once was, was now completely lost to me.

"Please tell me what happened." I pleaded. "Why am I here?" My voice sounded so shaky. I really just wanted to ask for the strongest pain medication they had but for some reason the other question seemed more appropriate.

"Chloe, you were in an accident a few nights ago and you're at Mass General," replied the doctor softly. "You were hit on the head and have amnesia. Your father here found you. When you came in you were in pretty rough shape and we had to do surgery to stop the bleeding vessels in your temporal lobe and prefrontal cortex. You also have some severe burns. I will give you some more morphine for the pain, which should hopefully help to comfort you some. They brought you to Boston hospital but your father had you transferred here. You should thank him, we really are the best at what we do and I'm not sure what would have happened had you gone somewhere else.

I watched him in fascination and relief as he hooked an IV up to my arm pumping me with miracle drugs. I really had no idea what he was talking about but at the moment I didn't really care. All that mattered to me was stopping the horrendous throbbing. I took a deep breath as I could feel the pain start to lessen. The doctor looked at me and I could tell that there were things he wasn't telling me. No one else seemed to be talking. Everyone seemed to be shifting from foot to foot not knowing what to say to me. So I just looked wide eyed at the doctor waiting for him to continue.

"Unfortunately," the doc started, "the police are here and need to ask you a few questions." They have been waiting all day for you to wake up. I've told them that there was little chance you would remember anything about the night right now but they seem to need to hear it for themselves. I know that this isn't easy, but do you think that you could gather up enough strength to talk to them? If it seems too much for you please let me know and I will send them away. Your health is my only concern right now."

"I guess I can talk to them," I said. In truth, I was doing my best to try to soak in what I had just heard. Now that the morphine was in my system I was beginning to feel sleepy but the pain didn't seem as intense. I was bone tired but little by little I could still begin to process a bit of what was going on. I felt like I was watching a play. Like I was watching a play and showed up in the middle of it. It was the strangest experience; I was just told the ending but what in the world was the beginning? This was not my life this doctor was talking about, it couldn't be. But what was my life? I could not muster up enough strength or think hard enough to figure that part out.

I glanced down and became aware that my body was covered in bandages. I quickly looked back up, I didn't want to look at myself, I just wanted to go to sleep. I needed to make the pain completely stop; this had to be a bad dream. No, this was worse than a bad dream this was a terrible nightmare.

"Don't worry, your mother, father, fiancé and I will be in the room to make sure that the police do not upset you too much," the doctor said, getting me to focus again on him. "It's very important to me that you do not over exert yourself. It's crucial to your recovery that you take it easy."

It was hard to focus though and I couldn't get my head to stop spinning. My mother, father and fiancé; I didn't remember any of these people. I wasn't sure if it was the morphine or the shock of everything that was happening but the dizziness kept getting more intense. I didn't feel strong enough to handle any of this. My supposed family and fiancé did not look like they approved of the two police officers as they walked in the room and I just couldn't comprehend why they were here to talk to me. I realized I didn't even know who I was. How could I help them when I couldn't figure out something as simple as my own name?

"Chloe, I know this is a lot to take in. The last thing we want to do is put any extra stress on your right now," said the first police officer, after introducing himself as Officer Perez. "We just need to know if you remember anything about the attack or the fire, or if you even remember why you were visiting your sister in the first place. Any information you can give us may help us find the person who put you here."

"Officer please," said my father. His eyebrows narrowed and a firm look took over his face. I realized what an intimidating looking man he was, bandaged up and all. It was the first time I really just looked at him. He seemed to have a presence that demanded respect. I wondered if he was a principal. He seemed as if he was an authority figure of some sort. Even the officers seemed sheepish in his presence. I couldn't help wondering what happened to him though. He must have been in some kind of accident. I realized it was possible and probable that he was in the same accident that put me in the hospital. The doctor did say that he was the one who found me. I turned my attention back to what he was saying to the officers. "We have not prepared her for all of this. Don't overwhelm her with questions. She doesn't remember anything."

Officer Perez seemed to be trying to stay in control although he did apologize to my father, calling him Judge. That answered my question on whether or not he was an authority figure. My father did not seem to phase him too much, but the other officer, whose badge read Officer Kellen, seemed like a nervous wreck, practically shaking while standing in front of my father.

I realized that everyone was looking at me and waiting for me to have some sort of response to the detective's questions. "My sister? I have a sister?" was the only response that came out of my mouth. "I was attacked?" I couldn't seem to take everything in, not to mention make sense of everything. Everything the officer was saying to me made no sense what so ever. At the same time, though, it made zero sense that I was even in the hospital room.

"Yes ma'am," said Officer Perez. "You were visiting your twin and the two of you were attacked inside her house. Your sister was shot and we assume that the attacker hit you on a head with some kind of metal object. It's also a possibility that you just fell and hit your head on something. After that, your attacker set the place on fire with some gasoline and matches. Lucky for you, your father found the two of you and got both of you out before the burns or the smoke inhalation took your life. We just have so many questions still and we were hoping that you would be able to help us fill in some of the blanks. If you could try your best to remember anything at all that would really help us out."

My fiancé all of sudden stopped his pacing of the room. "Officer! Did you not hear the Judge! Can't you tell she is in a vulnerable state! She needs to rest, not to be drilled!" His face was flushed in anger. His body seemed to shake in fury and it interested me because I felt no anger and I had just heard that I had been attacked. I could only feel confusion and pain. I was happy at least one of my questions was answered. My father must have received his injuries while pulling my sister and me out of the fire. This statement brought an even larger question to my mind.

"My sister, my twin sister.... I want to see her," was the response I managed in a hushed voice. Even though I asked, I was terrified to hear the response. I had a pain in my stomach, not from my injuries but from a strong sense of fear that swept over my body.

The whole room seemed to pause as everyone stared at me with a mixture of fear, pity and sadness in their eyes.

"I am afraid your sister died," replied the timid officer in a shaky soft voice.

The dizziness finally took over and as darkness enveloped me I heard my father screaming for the police to leave the room.

CHAPTER 1

5 YEARS LATER

"Chloe, where's my briefcase?" bellowed Kevin, the man that was my fiancé five years earlier. We were both frazzled due to the intense storm that pounded us the night before, blowing out the power and resulting in both of us waking up late. I knew that I should be happy that at least our power had returned and that there was no major damage done to our house, but it was hard when you felt like you were starting your day so far behind.

"It's beside the couch in the living room," I sighed back. He was an incredible man, driven and dangerously handsome: the kind of man that people paid to come listen to. Older people came to listen to his views on politics; while I, and People magazine, were convinced that the younger girls came not for his intellectual mind but for his movie star appearance. The combination of all of his assets is the reason that he is the youngest governor that Massachusetts has ever seen. It was amazing that he could remember new speeches on a weekly basis yet he could never seem to remember the location of where he had placed his briefcase just the night before.

"Thanks Darling," he said with a quick kiss on my check. "Have fun with the ladies, and I'll see you at the charity dinner tonight."

"You most certainly will," I said as I put on my new light green cashmere coat. As my husband walked away rapidly to get into his car where two men from his protection detail were waiting for him, I stepped outside and breathed in the cool ocean air. I knew I should hurry off since I was running late but I couldn't help but take a moment to stand and stare at the ocean. There was something so soothing about watching the rolling waves. I felt so fortunate that my husband had purchased this beautiful beachfront home on Commercial Street. I grew up in Provincetown, and while I do not recall my childhood there was something about this beach that felt so familiar and comfortable. I loved taking walks through the rocky sand during the day, searching for pretty pebbles to add to my collection at home. I also loved smelling the bonfires that the local teenagers and tourists built on the beach during the evening, it just felt like home. The ocean was at low tide and therefore the beach was littered with colorful seashells and ocean life that had swept up from the storm. I took a moment to enjoy the seagulls diving into the green blue ocean from the sky that showed no sign of the previous storm. As I stood taking in the moment of calm utter serenity I couldn't help but think back in amazement over everything that had occurred in the past five years.

My parents had to bury Breanna, my sister, without me due to my condition. It was a surreal thought to know that your sister was being buried. I knew it was happening and yet how do you mourn someone that you can't remember?

After a month in the hospital and some plastic surgery to take care of the burns, I was finally released and allowed to go home. It was a place that seemed so foreign to me. The doctor informed me that it was very likely that I would someday recover my memory. I have something called retrograde amnesia which is just a fancy way of telling me that I don't remember anything from my past or who I am. Some people lose their memory due to head injuries; others lose their memory because they have been through something so traumatic that their mind will not allow them to remember. It just happens that I had a head injury and a traumatic experience.

The doc said it wasn't impossible, but I would need to find the trigger that would allow my memories to resurface. I never did find that trigger even though I spent months looking at pictures. The pictures were amusing to me because after the plastic surgery I looked very different than the girl shown in the photos. Granted I was still a very pretty girl, and really do appreciate that the surgeon did an amazing job. There apparently were perks to coming from a very wealthy family: they had the money to get me the very best plastic surgeon. While I looked different, I was still a knock out; at least that's what Kevin and my friends say. I just don't look like the girl in the photos. My nose is shaped differently and my face has a new structure. It means absolutely nothing to me since I don't remember looking in the mirror and seeing another person, but at times I will see my mother or father steal a glance at me and I catch a glimpse of sadness in their eyes. I have secretly felt they have always felt guilty for that night. I think they feel responsible for not keeping me in Cape Cod and preventing me from being injured. I know rationally that is a ridiculous thought and I want to tell them to stop blaming themselves, but until they confide in me how they are feeling I can offer no consolation.

To help with my recovery, Kevin purchased this picturesque home in Cape Cod for us even though it is not traditional for the Governor to reside in Cape Cod. The doctor said that since this is where all of my memories are it would help me to stay in my hometown. It is lucky for me that the constituents of Massachusetts approve of the Governor residing in Cape Cod when it is for his wife's recovery. Therefore there has never been an issue with our home base being here, although Kevin does travel throughout the state quite a bit. Even though I still don't remember anything, I do love this town and would not want to be anywhere else in the world. There is nothing better then walking on the beach and down the streets of Provincetown. P-town, with its beautiful beaches and narrow streets has meant so much security for me, I feel safe and cocooned from the rest of the world here.

I couldn't help but think again how I am so thankful that Kevin thought to buy our house here. He has been very supportive in my recovery. I asked him once about our relationship B.A. (before accident) and he said we have always understood each other. Apparently our relationship hit a rocky patch at one point when Breanna told me she didn't like Kevin, but I guess she never liked any of my boyfriends so we were able to move past that pretty quickly. It made me sad to hear that she didn't like Kevin, but it is hard to be too upset about it when I still don't remember her or her reasons for not liking him. I am working towards remembering her, but it's frustrating because I feel like I have tried everything. I'm almost at the point of saying I am done trying to remember my past and instead just want to learn about my past and about the sister I don't remember so I can feel closer to my second half that is no longer here.

Through the past five years I have had my parents, Kevin and our friends telling me stories about my life hoping that I would remember. The police even hired a hypnotist in hope that he would be able to recover my memory of what I am assuming was the most horrifying night of my life. Nothing worked. It only left me frustrated, feeling out of place and all alone. It also left my family and friends feeling sad. They finally stopped trying to help me regain my memories and have asked me to just look forward at my bright future and forget about the darkness behind.

The most exasperating part of the whole thing is I know that I am missing something. I know there is something that I need to remember. It could be about the night or it could be about something else. I just don't know, and it appears that I never will. I have finally accepted that I will never remember my past, so I like to focus on my future.

The whole devastating night that the attack occurred is still one of the biggest mysteries that Massachusetts, especially Cape Cod, has ever known though. My family has been the talk of Cape Cod for decades but it was not until five years ago that the talk turned from everyone being envious of my family to those same people gossiping about my family, and more importantly, my twin sister.

According to what I have gathered over the past five years, Breanna had never really fit in with my family. She had always been somewhat rebellious. Not rebellious in the conventional manner, she just rebelled against being who my parents wanted her to be: me. She wanted nothing to do with the politics of Cape Cod or with my family. Apparently we were very close for years and then high school hit. During high school, our crowds separated and we became distant strangers. I became part of the "popular crowd" and she became more of a loner. Don't get me wrong, she did have friends. But instead of partying like my crowd did, they were more interested in having a quiet night watching a movie. She was not into fashion, drinking, drugs, or popularity. Due to this she was considered an outcast. The only reason people were tolerant of her was because she was my twin. From the stories that I have heard over the years, I tried to get her into my crowd but she had no desire to be my partner in running the school. Apparently Cape Cod and all of the people in it were just too much for her, because at the age of eighteen she left home. No one knows much about why she left, everyone just assumes it was because she did not fit in. It devastated my parents and they would prefer not to speak of her leaving to me or to anyone else.

When she left, no one knew where she went or what became of her life. At least that's what everyone thought. I knew where she lived, though, and I went there on the night of her death. The night I lost my identity, and any sense of who I am. Maybe I had just found out where she lived, maybe I had known for years. It is just one of the many questions that I will never be able to answer. But Breanna's story ends three years after she left, when I am mysteriously at her house, burned and knocked out and she is dead.

The only reason my father was able to track us down is because he was worried when I didn't show for our weekly dinner date. Apparently I have always been quite the daddy's girl and I never was late, or if I were going to be late I would call immediately and tell him where I was and when I would be arriving. I didn't answer my cell phone that night, though, when he called. He continually called me and as the night went on he began panicking. He could sense something was not right. He did tell me once that he has always assumed that I was planning on calling him once I left Breanna's to tell him I was running behind. He has friends in the police department and my cell phone has a tracking device. When he couldn't reach me, he made the call to them and demanded that they find me. The fact that he is a judge probably saved my life that night. Phone companies do not allow the police to track an individual using cell towers unless they believe a person is in danger. Someone not showing up to his or her parent's house for dinner is usually not cause to believe that a real danger exists. Since my father is a judge, no one at the police department wanted to tell him they believed he was being irrational. They tracked my phone, told my father where I was located. He found my car outside a burning house and went in to find both of his twin daughters inside.

Since then, my father has done anything and everything for me. It's like he is trying to make up for something. The only thing I can think of besides feeling guilty for not keeping me in Cape Cod is that he feels so guilty for Breanna running away, thinking he may have done something to cause her to leave. If she hadn't left she would probably still be alive today and I would still have my memory. It is ridiculous and my father has nothing to feel guilty for; he clearly loves me and he treasured Breanna. Still though, he does everything he can to make my life blissfully happy.

I am trying to get my life back to normal. I do everything that people told me that I did before, but I just feel like a fraud. I feel like I am living someone else's life. The ironic thing is that while I do feel like I am living out someone else's life, I have no idea what life I am supposed to live out. It just leaves me feeling discouraged and confused. My therapist has told me this is normal and I will continue to feel like this until I start to regain some of my old memories. She told me that all I can do now is focus on my future and stop putting all of my energy into remembering my past. When it is time for it to come back it will, but until then I should focus on my husband, friends and all of my activities. So, that is what I have been doing and what I will continue to do.

The strangest part of the whole thing is, even though I do not remember Breanna, I miss her. I miss her terribly. Twins are supposed to have a second sense of each other and I feel like I am missing a huge part of myself not having her around. My biggest fear is that I know what the trigger is to get my memory back. The trigger is my sister. The trigger died five years ago.

The sharp ring of my cell phone knocked me out of my deep thoughts. "Chloe! Are you almost here? The dinner is almost here and we have so much to do! To make matters worse, Raphael is still not here!"

"Tracy calm down," I said, turning my thoughts back to the present. I quickly turned from the ocean and hurried down the steps to my car parked on the circular drive. "Raphael had a family emergency and will be there at 10:00, and I am almost there." Tracy was one of the ladies that helped me plan the Black and White Charity Ball. It was an affair that *The Ladies of Cape Cod* planned every year. We were a group of socialites with a lot of money who chose to plan a variety of events throughout the year. Like all of the other ladies, I do love being a part of this group. The difference is: I love being A Lady of Cape Cod because it feels great to know that I am helping others out. The other ladies love being a member because it is a prestigious group. You have to receive an invitation to be in the group, something that I find lame. I say if you want to help others then you should be able to volunteer.

I pulled my white Jaguar up to the Provincetown Inn, a historic oceanfront resort at the far west end of P-Town and hurried inside as quickly as possible. I spotted my group running around making some final touches. "Hi girls," I yelled out to everyone with genuine smile. I might not fit in their group but I definitely loved the thought that we were really helping a good cause. All of the proceeds for the night would go to help underprivileged schools in inner cities.

"Chloe you will not believe it," said Stacy, one of the biggest gossips in the group. She quickly ran up to me and grabbed my arm. She pulled me aside like she had some big secret she had to share with me. Before I had a chance to respond she continued on. "Annabelle called and said she wanted to join *The Ladies of Cape Cod*! I couldn't believe it! I told her sweetly, of course, that we had no room for new members and maybe later, but really like we would ever have that piece of white trash be a part of our group!" she said flipping her perfectly dyed blond hair over her shoulder to reveal her new earrings. She said she deserved a splurge on herself when she bought the very expensive diamonds.

"Come on Stacy, she really isn't that bad," I said softly. I hated trashing people. I don't know if I was a trash talker before, but now I can't stand it. "Remember she was Breanna's best friend."

Stacy's face turned bright cherry tomato red. "Oh I am so sorry Chloe! I totally forgot. I meant no disrespect to Breanna."

"It's ok, they were friends a long time ago," I said with a little smile, trying to reassure her that I was not upset with her.

"That is true, Breanna would not be friends with her if she were around today," Stacy said with a satisfied nod.

I almost had to laugh. I couldn't believe the nerve of people, although she did have a point about Annabelle. Annabelle's mother was a cashier at a local liquor store and her father was a poor excuse for a mechanic, and while Annabelle was blessed with brains that got her scholarships to go to all of the same schools that I went to growing up, there was something about her that bothered me. I know that she and Breanna were best friends from Kindergarten until Breanna fled town. Who knows, maybe Breanna stayed in touch with her after she left town. And granted, I had only met Annabelle a hand full of times since the accident, but there was something about her that troubled me. It was not that her parents are not wealthy; it wasn't even really something I could put my finger on. I just for some reason or another did not like her.

"Hi friends," my best friend Lily said as she looped her arm in mine. "Stacy, I hope you don't mind, I really need to talk to Chloe about one of the centerpieces."

"Of course! I'll go make sure everything is going well in the kitchen. I've never trusted Chef Darren to get the job done."

I started chuckling as she hurried off. "Thank you so much, lifesaver!" I said, giving a hug to Lily. "That woman can be a real nightmare." Throughout everything I did feel so lucky to have Lily in my life. She sat with Kevin and me for hours right after the accident going over pictures and trying to help me regain my memory. She was my oldest friend and knew me better than almost anyone. I know my amnesia makes her sad; whenever she talks about something from the past that I can't remember I see a look flicker in her eyes. She quickly blinks it away and makes a fast joke. It's her defense mechanism. While I don't remember our friendship from the past, I definitely understand why she is my best friend. Loyal friends are hard to come by and when you find a good one you cherish it.

I hugged my best friend one more time, taking a moment to appreciate the great things I had in my life. If I was never going to regain my memory then at least I had great friends to teach me about my past and be a part of my future. "Come on Lily, let's get this event put together before the guests arrive."

Chapter 2

The day went by fast with final vases being placed and final instructions given out, and before I knew it, it was 4:00 and time for me to head home and get ready for the beautiful night. I quickly showered and put on my black backless Valentino dress. As I put my white gloves on, I looked in the mirror and had to admit that even though people tell me that I'm not the same girl I once was I was not a bad looking woman.

The Cape Cod Life Magazine once described me as a sight that would take your breath away. While everyone around me seems to breath just fine, I know that I am not sore on the eyes. My hair grew back even thicker and blonder than it was before the accident and before they had to shave my head for my surgery. I grew it long and it fell past my shoulders. My eyes were a piercing royal blue color; something my twin and I shared and something that the accident did not change. Looking at old photos it was nice to see something that looked the same about me.

After the accident my muscles were very weak due to weeks of bed rest, but even though it took awhile I managed with hard work and a great trainer to regain my muscle strength. Now, even though I was short at 5'2, I was not a damsel in distress and I was stronger than I looked. It also gave me a great figure. Many of the women in *The Ladies of Cape Cod* were constantly telling me how jealous they were of my figure. The jealousy made me laugh every time, anyone could have a decent figure. Any of those women could afford the same trainer that I had used. I was jealous of them. They didn't have a huge gap in their life. There was nothing I could do to fix that.

Besides all of that though, I am also quite successful in my own way. In the past five years I received a diploma from Harvard University in business management and since then I have become very involved around Cape Cod helping out with a list of local charities.

"You look incredible," Kevin said as he stood in the doorway. He quickly came over and gave me a kiss on the cheek. "But no time to admire you now, we have to leave. It would look terrible for the hostess to show up late," he said, ushering me out of the doorway.

"You're right," I said, with a small smile on my face. I knew even if he had time to admire me he wouldn't. We were a beautiful couple but I could not remember when we last enjoyed ourselves in the bedroom and there was always a distance between us. I was so grateful to him for all of his support in my time of need. I know he loves me. That has never been a question, but I had wondered on more then one occasion if he was cheating on me. I even approached my father about the issue on one occasion but he dismissed it with a wave of his hand. "Kevin loves you, he is crazy about you," he replied. My father is extremely fond of Kevin. He is a retired judge and appreciates where Kevin came from, another well known political family. He also loves the prestige of having a governor as a son-in-law. So after he answered me I didn't have the nerve to reply that yes he does love me but that doesn't necessarily mean that he isn't cheating on me. Plenty of adoring husbands stray and cheat on their wives. In the five years of memories that I have, I know numerous women who have gotten divorces for that reason. I decided not to pursue my fears though. Some may call me stupid and weak but at the end of the day I have been through enough and right now I like the comfort of nothing else changing. Plus, Kevin does for the most part make me happy. It may not be the most intimate marriage but it is a decently happy life.

Kevin quickly guided me to the car and we were off in our car, sandwiched in between our security which tonight consisted of one car leading and another one following. "Who are we sitting with?" he asked casually. He loved to be informed of these things before hand so he could make a good impression during the meal. He was known for even researching people before events. If they loved him there was a good chance they would contribute to his next campaign and, as everyone knows, fundraising is the most important part of a politician's campaign.

"Well I placed our parents at another table so we could mingle with some new people. We will be with Sandi Bowen, who works with some of the inner city schools, along with her husband Bill. She invited a few people who also work with inner city schools. Also, of course, we will be with Mayor Taylor and his wife. Other than that, just a few of the ladies who helped plan the event with me and their husbands. Unfortunately Lily and Don will be at another table since we already have dinner with them almost once a week.

"Well that sounds like a good mix even without Lily and Don, it will look good for the next campaign," he said with a firm look of approval. I sighed; he couldn't even pretend that everything didn't revolve around his next campaign. I often spent time dreaming of the day when he is retired from the spot light and we could just indulge in everything life has to offer. For now, I would even be satisfied with one conversation that didn't someone how turn to talk about the campaign.

We pulled up to the valet and walked to the door, stopping to smile at some of the cameras that were outside taking photos. A few of the local papers came out to get a peak at the Governor with his wife. I am sure Kevin's people made sure everyone knew we were here. Although, since I was an organizer, I guess it would have been assumed we would both be in attendance.

We walked into the elegantly decorated ballroom and I smiled to myself. We had done a fantastic job. Maybe in my last life I was an event coordinator. That thought made me laugh out loud, I was speculating about my previous life and I could not even remember my current one.

"Well it looks like you are having a great time already," said my mom as she and my dad approached us.

I felt my cheeks turn a little crimson, "Oh just lost in my thoughts."

"Kevin, how about you and I go to the bar and grab the ladies some drinks" my dad said after he gave me a quick kiss on the cheek and then motioned for Kevin to follow him.

"Oh Chloe, we are so proud of you," my mom beamed. "We know how hard you worked on this event and it looks magnificent."

"Thanks mom," I said, genuinely pleased that she approved of the event. I always felt like there was something distant between the two of us. Now don't misunderstand, I loved my mother, she was my rock when I was recovering in the hospital but I always felt like there was something genuine missing from her. It felt like she was always putting on a façade. Maybe she was. She had been through a lot of pain in her life and yet always had a smile on her face. Everything that had happened, from Breanna running away to the night of her death had to have broken her more than just a little. Yet you would never know it. The only time I had seen her waiver even a little was the first night I woke up in the hospital before she noticed me watching her. She is the strongest person I know or have even known; I just wish I could feel more of a connection to her. I guess I was just a daddy's girl and maybe everyone felt more of a connection to one parent.

"Well I am going to go say hello to the Mayor and his wife. You have a good time tonight, you did all of the work, now relish in its results!"

I did have a good time and the rest of the night was very pleasant. After we were all seated at our tables I got to talk to Sandi Bowen some and found that she is a very sweet woman and that her friends were all very pleasant. It wasn't until she offered a challenge that the night got interesting. "Chloe, have you ever visited an inner city school before?"

That question kind of took me off my guard. "Well actually no, but I would love to do everything I can do to help," I replied genuinely.

"The first thing that you could do would be to visit some inner city schools one day. Really see what you are working with. It will give you an idea of what they need."

"I think that is a great idea," said Kevin. "I'll accompany you and we'll make a day out of it," he decided as he took a sip of his scotch.

"Are you kidding?" I said with a laugh. "with how busy you are? I'll be happy to do it though., My husband is ambitious with his time but I know how demanding his schedule is right now but I do have some free time now that this event is over and I would love to do a visit whenever you think it would be appropriate," I replied to Sandi without looking at Kevin. I am sure he wore a heavy scowl on his face. I knew he would like to come with me, but charity had always been my thing and I would like to do this on my own. Plus, I knew his schedule was way overbooked.

"Well how about Tuesday? I know of a perfect man that could show you around!" exclaimed Sandi. "Detective Trevor Cading has always been a huge advocate for increasing funding of our inner city schools. I know he has Tuesday off and I'm sure he would love to be your escort. I would do it but I think you will be safer with the Detective as your guide."

I felt a huge shiver go down my spine for no apparent reason. I seemed to freeze all of a sudden and I could not reply or for that matter make any kind of movement. My mind felt strained as if it was trying to remember something that it could not.

At the same moment Kevin nearly chocked on his whiskey. When he finally recovered, claiming it went down the wrong pipe, he brought the table back to the conversation on schools.

"Safe? Why would she not be safe," Kevin replied.

"These schools have some tough children in them." Sandi said, "It's always a good idea to have an officer with you when going through them, unfortunately. School today is not like it was ten years ago. Just last week a teacher was sent to the hospital because a girl pushed her down the stairs. It's all about home environment and unfortunately most of these kids come from very rough homes. That's why we are trying to raise money, so we can begin working towards a better school environment."

"That's terrible!" Kevin said in a shocked voice. "I don't know if I like the idea of my wife going into such an unsafe atmosphere," he said with false alarm in his voice. It would be bad for his image if he didn't play the concerned husband.

"You have nothing to worry about," Sandi said. "I have known Trevor for a couple of years and he will definitely make sure that Chloe is safe."

"Well, I don't know this Trevor and I do not want some man I do not know to take my wife around," Kevin said insistently with extreme annoyance.

"All right," I managed to say in a strained voice. "I would love to come, where are the schools?"

"Chloe this is a bad idea!" Kevin said, as his voice raised a decibel.

I gave him a bewildered look. "Kevin, I am a grown woman who will be escorted by a Detective who Sandi trusts. I will be fine," I said shutting him down.

His face flushed with embarrassment, and he tried to redeem his image, "Well you know a husband can never be too worried about his wife," he said with in a resigned voice. I wondered if everyone else could tell how fake he was. Plastic, was a good way to describe him. I remember sitting in my room watching the movie Mean Girls one day and hearing them describe the girls as plastic and I went into an uncontrolled fit of giggles because it reminded me of my husband. How fake he always was with everyone, and it was like he always had a plastic smile on his face. It cracked me up that night while I sat in bed with a bowl of popcorn in my lap comparing my handsome successful husband to a group of high school girls. That memory brought a smile to my face and I felt myself start to relax again. I had no idea why I had the pang of panic, visiting the school would be fun. My smile brought a bigger smile to Kevin's face. He obviously thought I was smiling in agreement to his comment.

"Well then it is settled, she will go and I will just make sure Trevor watches over her closely," Sandi said with a firm nod of her head. This brought an unexpected frown from Kevin. He was really over-playing this protective husband bit. Granted, in some ways he was protective of me. I always felt in some ways like a possession to him. I was his trophy wife meant for him to do with as he pleased. But good grief, this would look good for his campaign if I went to this school. What was his deal?

The schools were in Boston and I managed to set up the details with Sandi. Later, as Kevin and I lay in bed, on our separate sides of course, I continued to run that name through my head. Trevor Cading, it sounded so familiar for some reason, as if in my heart I knew it meant something to me. I most certainly was going to find out on Tuesday.

The next two days went by slowly. I did the usual meet and greets with Kevin and did my usual workouts and manicure with Lily. Kevin had hardly said a word to me since the charity ball, minus to tell me that I should never go against what he says in front of people again.

I told Lily about what had happened and she rolled her eyes, "Kevin can be so controlling, but I am sure he doing it because he loves you. Don't you worry though, as designated best friend I have your back! If you want I can claim I wanted you to go and you were just trying to be a good friend."

"Thanks Lily! Not necessary though, I need to save the DBF card for something more useful then keeping my husband happy," I said laughing as we walked around one of the cute antique stores in town.

"Ok, but remember keeping husbands happy is a full time job, trust me I know!" she said laughing. Lily is married to Kevin's campaign manager, Don Gregory. She is constantly thanking me; I apparently introduced them before the accident when Kevin and Don were just really good friends. Don always jokes with me about how you can't not love Lily; if I chose her for my best friend then she must be fabulous. A few of the ladies around town have gossiped that they do not know what Don sees in Lily. Don's looks mirror Kevin's. In fact, many people mistake them for brothers. Both are blond with blue eyes and both are around 6 foot tall with muscular bodies. Lily, on the other hand, looks nothing like me. She is brunette, around 5'6, wears glasses, and while she is skinny, her figure lacks the curves that I have been blessed with. Many women call her appearance mousy. Whenever I over hear anyone say anything about her, though, my inner tigress comes out and I quickly put them in their place. Don loves Lily for exactly the reasons I do. She is loyal, funny and a fantastic woman. Their marriage has even helped Kevin and my marriage by the mere fact that it is wonderful to have another couple that both of us love spending time with.

I left Lily, giving her a quick hug, and got into my car. Immediately my mind wandered back to my fight with Kevin. He was not going to tell me not to go now, because it would look bad when people were expecting me to be there. I could tell something was making him nervous though. I couldn't place my finger on what it was. When I pulled into the driveway it hit me that maybe he was actually worried about me and I had just gotten too used to second guessing him over the years. Once that thought hit my mind I started to rethink our whole fight. I actually started to think maybe he was just being sweet to me. I finally decided he was not playing and he was actually concerned about me. That night I moved over to his side of the bed.

"Honey?' I said softly, not sure if he was still awake.

"Hmm," he said.

"I am sorry I'm going tomorrow. I didn't realize how upset it would make you. I promise next time you don't want me to go somewhere I wont just dismiss your opinion."

"Well as long as we got that settled," he said in a rough voice, clearly waking up from a half sleep. He rolled on his back and pulled me on top of him. We made love that night for the first time in a very long time.

When Tuesday rolled around I could hardly stand it. I was so excited to go to Boston. I left early, careful not to wake Kevin. I had to leave around 5:00AM so I could make it to Boson by the beginning of the school day at 7:00. I tried not to speed, which ended up being easy with the heavy traffic. You would think that early in the morning traffic would be a breeze but Boston was never that simple and I ended up getting caught up and arrived just on time. Sandi was waiting for me in her office. I introduced myself to her secretary and was ushered into Sandi's office. I could see that a man was sitting across from her with his back facing me. "Good morning," I said cheerfully ready to start my day.

"Good morning Chloe! I would like you to meet Lieutenant Cading. The lieutenant stood slowly and turned to me with a very intense expression. I could almost feel my heart stop. As I looked at his masculine features, and most importantly into eyes, I could hardly breathe. I knew he some how held part of the key to what had happened five years prior. My heart stopped and the room spun as I collapsed with the knowledge that something huge was about to unravel.

CHAPTER 3

"Chloe wake up," I prodded. "Please, open your eyes," I said fanning her with a sheet of paper.

"I can't believe this, what do you think is wrong with her? I should call a doctor. You know she has been through a lot. I heard through the grapevine that five years ago she was attacked and maybe she is still having issues from that," Sandi said babbling as fast as she possibly could.

"Sandi she will be fine in a minute, why don't you go get her some water," I said cutting her off. "It's hot in here; the heat must have just gotten to her," I continued in a tense voice. I had not expected the meeting to start out this way. When Sandi had asked if I would show Chloe around I wanted to scream as loud as I could "No," I could not stand to see the woman that looked identical to Breanna. There was not a day that went by that I did not miss Breanna and wish that she was still here. Even though she died five years ago, it still felt like it was just yesterday.

Instantly when Sandi said Chloe's name, my mind flashed to my last morning with Breanna. I was not in the best mood due to waking up late and cutting my face shaving. I ran into the kitchen to grab a to-go mug of coffee and there she stood. Somehow she always looked beautiful no matter what time of day it was. She stood there holding my mug of coffee and a paper bag with a homemade muffin in it. "Don't think I was going to let you sneak out without some breakfast. It is the most important meal of the day and I need my big strong cop to be fueled up for his day of fighting crime," Breanna smirked. She always popped me out of my bad mood. I decided being late was worth it and carried my giggling Bre into the bedroom. It ended up being one of the smartest decisions I ever made, because that was the last time I got to be with her.

Most people tiptoed around talking about Breanna or her family to me. Sandi was not aware of my relationship to the family, though, which is why it did not seem like a big deal to ask me to show Chloe around. When she asked, I felt like someone had punched me in the gut and all the wind went out of my lungs. I just wasn't sure if I could emotionally take looking at my dead wife's twin.

After some thought though, I remembered what I had read. She had a lot of plastic surgery, and while the news praised the plastic surgeon, it apparently had altered her looks quite drastically. So I figured I could give seeing her a shot, maybe it would be so bad. Plus, I couldn't go the rest of my life fearing that one day I would run into her. Besides, she probably doesn't even know that Breanna had been married. I am sure her sleazy husband knew, and that the son-of-a-bitch father of hers' knew as well. At one point in time Chloe knew about our marriage but with her memory loss I assume that the subject had never been brought up. In fact the opposite of that, I am sure that the subject was avoided completely.

Her father had made sure that I sat in the back of the church at the funeral and that my name was never mentioned to anyone. The Judge had a strong hatred for me since he blamed me for Breanna never coming back home. I tried to call him once to introduce myself. I thought that if I could speak to him maybe I could help mend things between Breanna and her family. He was shocked and disgusted that I called. After some unpleasant words, he simply asked me never to call him again and hung up the phone. I never told Breanna about that conversation because I didn't want to upset her, but after that day I never wanted anything to do with him.

But Chloe was different than her father, as Breanna had been. Breanna always believed that deep down Chloe was a good person living in a life full of lies. From what I understood, though, Chloe was definitely not like Breanna. From everything I had heard she was stuck up, fake and a bitch. She was not devious though, nothing like the Judge and the Governor. At least that is what Breanna said.

God, I missed my wife. It hit me like a ton of bricks. I had not expected taking a glimpse into Chloe's eyes would affect me like that. Looking into those eyes, my wife's eyes, eyes that the surgery hadn't changed, was a huge blow. I don't know why I didn't prepare myself mentally for that. Surgery would of course not alter someone's eyes and I knew that Chloe and Breanna had been identical in all physical ways. I thought I had remembered everything about Breanna, but somehow I forgot how I felt looking into her eyes. How could I have forgotten the twinkle of excitement that showed when Breanna was ready to take on anything and everything? When I felt frustrated or agonized from whatever my day held I would just take one look into those eyes and the twinkle would fill me with exhilaration and always lifted my spirits.

When Chloe walked in I felt like I had been punched hard in the stomach. She might have changed a lot but she still reminded me of my beloved. I knew that Breanna had sent pictures of me to her and was surprised that seeing me had jolted her memory. When she walked in her voice sounded so happy and calm and when I turned and looked at her, her entire face changed to shock.

Slowly, her eyes opened and her eyelashes fluttered with the same surprised look. "I know you," she whispered with a slight tremble.

"I know," I whispered back gently as I sat her up. "We will talk about it later." With that, Sandi walked back in with a glass of water and a medical kit. She still appeared frazzled and was obviously still upset and worried about Chloe.

"Chloe would you like me to call a doctor?"

"No I'm fine," she said as her cheeks started to regain color and turned slightly rosy. "I am so embarrassed about that. I don't know what happened. I guess I just got hot and felt light headed. I just need some water and fresh air. But I am ready to get looking at these schools," she said as she sat up and smoothed out the wrinkles of her black slacks. Color was now fully returning to her face and she appeared to have a handle of herself again.

"Are you sure," Sandi asked with hesitation in her voice as she handed her the glass of water. "After everything you have done for us the last thing I want to do is put you in any kind of jeopardy. Plus, I did promise the Governor that I would make sure you were safe and well watched over.

"I will make sure she is ok," I said as I helped her to her feet. "My car is parked out back," That seemed to end the conversation and Chloe said her goodbyes to Sandi and I quickly helped her to the car. To make sure she was not still dehydrated, I handed her a bottle of water and then awaited her questions as I hopped into the driver seat.

"I know I know you," she said quietly with confusion in her voice. The voice broke my heart. It sounded so much like the voice I woke up to every day for two years. She sat there for a minute clearly racking her brain trying to solve the mystery. She had the same look that I would get whenever I was close to figuring out some big case. "When Kevin and I were dating, were we involved?" she asked.

I had to choke back my astonishment. "No!" I nearly shouted. I couldn't believe how far off base she was. I apologized quickly when I saw her startled, embarrassed expression. In a more gentle tone, I explained, "I was married to your sister." Her face filled with absolute shock.

"What, but no one ever said, I mean I don't understand."

"Your father knows about me, and I wouldn't be shocked if you husband does too, but everyone else in Cape Cod had no idea. We married when she was 19 and I was 24. We were only married for two years before she passed away. We made our life here, filled it with close friends and my family," I said trying to explain.

I glanced over at her and saw a hurt expression and realized I needed to explain a little further. "I know she sent you a letter once with my picture in it. She missed you terribly, but did not feel as if she could return to her family.

I wish I could tell you why, but she did not like to go into details and I never pushed it. Anytime I asked she would just get upset. She always said put the past in the past and focus on the future, our future."

Chloe sat quietly, obviously soaking in all of this information about her dead sister. "Did you go to her funeral?" she asked softly.

"Yes," I replied quietly. "Your father insisted on being the one to plan the details of the funeral and asked me not to make a scene and just to sit towards the back, since your mother never knew about me. He felt it was respectful towards her. Plus, he never liked me. He never knew me but he decided not to like me. To this day I regret that, I should be allowed to shout to everyone how much we loved each other."

"My father is very protective of his family. I am sure he didn't mean to hurt you. He just wanted to do what he could to protect my mom. But yes, you are right you should have been able to tell everyone. Breanna should not have kept your marriage from our mother. I guess it's hard for me to understand why she would have kept it a secret." She looked down at the floorboard seemingly lost in thought. She was twirling of her hair around her finger, just like her sister used to when she was lost in though.

"I don't think she was trying to keep us a secret," I said, as gently as possible not wanting to upset her anymore. "She just didn't want your parents to be a part of her life. I don't know why she made that decision but she was adamant about it. I told her that one day she was going to have to tell me everything that had happened that caused her to run, but I didn't want to push her and make her tell me before she was ready."

Do you know who killed her," she asked lifting her head and hitting me those piercing blue eyes. I did everything in my power not to look into them.

"No, and it rips me apart everyday. I have searched and searched and can't figure out what happened that day. I was kept off the case, but I read every report and talked to the investigating detectives all the time. I just wish I'd pushed and made her open up to me. I was her husband. She should have told me why she left home in the first place, and why you were visiting her that day." I felt my voice start cracking but I knew I had to keep it together for Chloe. I live with this everyday but this must be so much for her to learn and take in, all at once.

"I want to find out the truth," she said with a firmness and strength that surprised me. "I didn't realize how much until right now. It's crazy I didn't even know that my sister was married. How messed up is my life that the people I trust and love feel that they have to shield me from everything including my brother-in-law. I want answers. It's sad I can't trust the people I love to give me those answers but if I can't get the answers from them then it's time I start looking for them. I want to know who I am and god dammit, I want to know who took my sister from me!" she said in a soft voice that put a chill in me. "I want to know who stole my memories and my sense of identity. I want answers and I think I have the right to them. Regardless of what everyone else might think.

"OK," I said finally finding the strength to look at her again. She had the same uncompromising resolute look that Breanna got whenever she had made up her mind about something. I knew the look well and understood what it meant. Chloe was going to begin to search for the same answers I had been searching for nonstop for the past five years. I realized that there was only one thing I could do. I had to do what Breanna would have wanted me to do, which was to keep her sister safe. "Chloe", I said reminding myself who I was speaking with, "we'll find out. You're not alone in this anymore. I need those answers too. Remember you're not the only person who lost something that night. I lost my best friend, the love of my life and the woman who was supposed to be the mother of my children. Anything you need I am here and I want to help you."

"Thank you," she said, her voice full of gratitude and surprise. I realized that I am probably the first person who didn't try to stop her questioning in a long time. Knowing her family, they probably accepted her memory loss and decided that they needed to move forward and focus on politics and not their messy family history.

We pulled up to the school a minute later, which stopped our conversation from going any farther. Chloe walked through the school focused on what she was doing. She took notes on every little thing and asked a million questions. It shocked me. She was not at all what or who I expected her to be. I guess I should not have believed everything I had read. Breanna always told me she was sweeter than the tabloids made her out to be. I should have believed her. It was just hard when I knew how Breanna gave everyone the benefit of the doubt and chose to see the best in people. It was uncanny though; Chloe was so similar to Breanna. The only big difference I could see is that Chloe didn't have that rebellious fire my wife had. Granted it had been five years and people do change. Maybe Chloe had been a little bit more like how the tabloids pictured her five years ago and due to the accident, or even just time, she had grown up and realized what was important in life.

In studying her further, there was actually something kind of sad about Chloe. You could tell she didn't want to display any vulnerability but there was something there, in her eyes, that gave away how she felt. She had such a lost look about her. Even when her face filled with determination, which happened any time she noticed something else that could be done to improve the school, there was still something there that just kind of showed that pieces were missing from her life and she wasn't sure where she belonged.

We were finishing up the day when Josh Turner, the school principal, asked to speak with me in his office.

"Josh, is this something that can wait," I asked eyeing Chloe.

"Don't be silly, Trevor" Chloe said with a light smile. "I don't mind waiting for you. Plus I want to read these articles on the wall," she said referring to the newspaper articles Josh had framed about the school pushing for a new Science wing.

"Alright," I said. "If any kid gives you any trouble just yell for me."

"Sure thing," she said waving me off as she already turned her focus to the first article.

"Trevor," Josh said as we entered his office. "I just wanted your opinion on a new security system we were considering installing." He laid out the information over the new advanced cameras and alarms. As I studied the documents, I heard a voice start yelling. It was Chloe.

Chapter 4

As Trevor entered the principal's office a bell rang through the air. I frowned to myself because I wanted to remember my high school days. What was my favorite class, who was my favorite teacher? They are questions that my friends have told me the answers to, but still it seems like they are talking about someone I never even met.

"Hola, mamasita," a skinny teenage boy with bad acne said tearing my thoughts away from me. He was Hispanic, wearing pants that seemed to bag down to his knees and a backwards hat. I'm surprised the school didn't have a dress code. Something I should talk over with Josh. A dress code teaches teenagers how they should dress once they are out in the real world trying to obtain decent jobs.

The boy obviously thought quite highly of himself. He was looking me up and down as he got closer. "What's a fine mama like you doin standin here all by yaself," he said clearly trying to sound as gangster as possible. Then it occurred to me that maybe he was in a gang. I was extremely naïve to that world but I had watched the news enough and viewed enough of the statistics that came across Kevin's desk that I knew that gangs were beginning to be a real problem in some schools – just another issue to discuss with Josh. There are so many great anti-gang protocols that are being implemented in high schools across the country. There's no reason that this school could not take some initiative and implement some of those protocols right here.

Turning my attention back to the student, I replied, ignoring his "fine mama" comment. "I am waiting for my detective friend who's been escorting me to come out of the office to finish my tour of this facility." I kept a smile on my face and I turned my head back to the article that I had just begun to read.

"Girl, I think I should give you the tour," he said grabbing my arm spinning me around. He was getting so close that I could smell the tobacco on his breath as he backed me up against the wall. I could feel my body go rigid as I looked at the office door wondering if I should call out to Trevor. I looked over his shoulder and could see a couple of his buddies snickering as they watched him harass me.

"Excuse me!" I said angrily. "Do not grab my arm and please back up, you are crowding me. I am a married woman," I said, holding up my left hand so he could see my ring. "Plus," I added to make a point, "I am much too old for you and would appreciate it if you would leave me alone!"

"Ah, but baby I like older women and I ain't scared of your husband," he said as he pushed me hard against the wall.

"Stop it now," I said raising my voice to a scream. "Back up and leave me alone!" He was about to respond when he was thrown away from me and Trevor was standing in between the two of us as his buddies quickly ran off away from the scene.

"Are you bothering this nice lady," Trevor said with a growl to his voice.

"Marcus, my office now!" bellowed Josh.

As Marcus walked away from us, still looking me up and down obviously not nervous or at all troubled by Trevor, Trevor turned towards me. "Are you ok?" he said, his face full of concern. I felt like his eyes were burning into mine and all of sudden I became very conscious of the crowded hallway full of students looking in my direction. "I'm fine," I said, tucking my hair behind my ear while my eyes darted around the hallway trying to avoid Trevor's very serious expression. "Who raises these kids? I mean I know that teenagers rebel but I cannot imagine acting that way when I was their age," I said, then stopping to realize that I really had no idea how I acted in high school.

"All right," he said backing up some but keeping his hard gaze on my face searching for any sort of injury. "I think the tour is over for today."

We said our goodbyes to a couple of teachers and headed to the car. As soon as we got in Trevor started driving in the opposite direction of where my car was parked.

"Where are we going?" I asked. "My car is at parked in the garage at Sandi's office building."

"I know," he said. "I thought we could go to lunch. You need to eat; I don't want you passing out again. Plus, it will give us a little bit of time to finish up our last discussion."

I didn't object because I really did want to talk about my sister some more. I still couldn't get over that she was married and I was sitting next to her husband; her extremely handsome husband. Who seemed to be deeply in love with her. I had not really studied him back in Sandi's office because I was so dazed and shocked over finally recognizing someone. I didn't know how I knew him but I knew that I recognized him and that was huge. It was the first time I felt like a memory was trying to come back. As I sat in his car I had the chance to really study him because he was focused on the road. He was handsome in a dark, masculine, rough way. He had dark brown hair and dark brown eyes, a rough square chin and two dimples that seemed to mysteriously appear along with a spark in his eyes when he smiled.

He turned his head as he noticed me studying him. I quickly turned my head to look out my window as I felt my face flush, embarrassed that he caught me looking at him. "I should not be checking him out," I thought, scolding myself. This is ridiculous, I love Kevin and he is my sister's husband!

The thought of Kevin instantly brought a flash of anger; I was extremely pissed at him. He obviously knew that Trevor was Breanna's husband. He was never worried about me he was just afraid I would find out about Trevor. How dare he! What gave him the right to decide what information I should know about my own family. Why would he not want me to find out about my sister's husband? Whatever the reason was I would definitely find out when I got home.

"Penny for your thoughts," Trevor said as we pulled into a parking lot of a small diner that had a massive sign on top in the shape of a coffee cup.

"Sorry," I replied softly, not sure if I was talking to him or to myself. "I just don't know why my father and Kevin never told me about you."

"Well, as I said before, your father never liked me, which means your husband probably doesn't like me either. I guess it makes sense that they wouldn't tell you about me," he said slowly. "If they had, then you would probably want to meet me. I mean it would only make sense; I would be a link to your twin. Then I would be back in their lives and to them, that would just be terrible," he finished dryly.

"But why," I persisted. "Why wouldn't they want me to meet you? And what possible reason could they have had not to like you. You're successful and respected; two big pluses in my father's books."

"He blames me," he replied simply and without any expression. "He thinks I'm the reason that Breanna never went home." Before I had a chance to say anything else he hopped out of the car and walked around to open my door.

We entered the small diner and grabbed a booth next to the window. A woman looking to be in her sixties approached the booth immediately after we sat down. She looked incredibly irritated and reeked of cheap perfume mixed with cigarette smoke.

"What can I get the two of you," she asked in a hoarse voice, not glancing up at us once. We quickly opened the menus and made our selections. We both ordered iced teas and tuna sandwiches.

"Well we both want to know what happened that night, the question is how do we find out," I said mostly thinking out loud.

"Well I think a good place to start would be to find out why you came to visit."

"That's probably as good a place as any but I've been trying to figure that out for the past five years but I got nothing. And it seems I never told anyone why I was going there. Wait, was that my first time going there? Do you know?" I asked, kind of excited that at least one question would get answered.

"Yea, it was," he said, then shrugged his shoulders. "I mean, at least that I know of, and I don't think that Breanna would have kept it from me if you had been there before. From what I understand you didn't come to our house spontaneously; the two of you had arranged to meet there. I found a note in her planner about you coming. When I saw the note I was surprised she didn't tell me, but I am guessing she would have told me about it later. We usually recapped our days to each other over a drink after work." He gave a little smile at the memory then focused back on the conversation.

"You guys didn't communicate much. You would occasionally talk on the phone and she wrote to you to tell you that we were married, but you were always just so angry with her for leaving. You felt she abandoned you. I know she wanted to make it up to you but she just didn't know how to do that."

"Why did she leave?" I asked even though he had already mentioned he didn't know. Maybe he knew more than he thought he did. Regardless, he knew more than I knew, including what Breanna was like and what the last two years of her life were like.

"That's one thing I never knew the answer to. As I said, I would ask her over and over again but she would always clam up and change the subject. She said that it was a part of her past and she just wanted to focus on the future," he said with bitterness to his voice.

Everything he said stung my heart. It was too hard to hear it all; from learning that I was not as close to my sister as I had thought and hoped, to hearing my sister's husband's pain at losing his chance for his future with her. Everything just made my desire to find out what happened even stronger. If my family didn't tell me about Trevor and Breanna they may have kept other secrets from me as well. They wouldn't have done it viciously but to try to protect me. They were always trying to protect me. They seemed to think if they said one wrong thing I would just break. What they did not realize, though, is that I am a lot stronger than people give me credit for. I have been through a ton in the past five years and I am still standing and still going. Many people would have cracked but I persevered.

Our food came and we ate in silence for the next few minutes. "Well, so what should we do," I asked finally, placing my half eaten sandwich down. I always had issues eating when I had a ton on my mind. With everything that had happened today it would be amazing if I could really eat much of anything for the next week.

"I think we need to piece together that whole day, starting with talking to your friends, parents and Kevin. Find out if you told them anything about your conversation with Breanna that day."

"That is going to be easier said than done," I said. "I asked so many questions about that night when I was released from the hospital and no one would tell me anything. Well, at least nothing with any more details than what everyone already knew. They just all kept tiptoeing around me. It wasn't until I got back to what they decided was normal that people started to act comfortable around me. Anytime I bring up Breanna or that night they tell me that talking about it isn't going to bring back my memories and I am just upsetting everyone by bringing it up," I said, partly to myself as I crumpled up a napkin mindlessly.

"That must have been very hard for you," he said, covering my hand that held the now shredded napkin with his. "To be alone trying to understand everything. I want to help you. It won't be easy to get everyone to open up to you but I'm confident that you can do this."

I gave Trevor a small smile. "Its amazing that you're so confident in something that I really have no confidence in. What are you going to do while I do this," I asked looking down at his hand covering mine.

"I'll make copies of the police report from that night and bring it to you, see if anything strikes you odd. I've read the report a million times but maybe something will jump out to you," he said, quickly removing his hand taking back the intimacy of the moment.

The rest of the meal went well. We got away from talking about the attack and began talking about movies, books and a whole bunch of other random topics. It felt like we've know each other forever. Talking to him was so easy. I could easily see why my sister had fallen in love with him and it seemed hard to imagine that the rest of my family would not embrace him. He is family after all, and even though we lost Breanna at least we can get to know her husband. I understand it will be hard for my mother to accept that her daughter did not invite her to her wedding but I really felt like once she met Trevor she would think he was great and welcome him with open arms.

We agreed to meet a week from today on his next day off. We decided on a more private setting, his apartment. That way we wouldn't be spotted together and possibly cause bad press for Kevin, plus it would give us the privacy we needed to discuss such a sensitive subject. By the time we left we realized it was getting late. We had been in the café for the better part of the afternoon. Trevor left a big tip on the table as an apology to the waitress for taking up her table for so long and drove me back to my car. As I reached my car I realized that Kevin would be pissed at me for running late.

"Feel free to call me if anything comes up that you would like to talk about," Trevor said. He leaned in, handed me his card and grazed his lips across my check. I shivered and quickly said goodbye before I had anymore inappropriate thoughts about this man who my sister had clearly loved so deeply and so passionately that she decided he would be her new family.

As I was driving home through the horrendous Boston traffic I picked up my cell phone and hit speed dial number one.

"Hello beautiful," Kevin answered, with a nervous strain to his voice.

"So when were you planning on telling me about my brother-in-law Trevor Cading?" I replied ignoring everything else he was saying to me.

Chapter 5

I woke in the morning with a nervous knot in my stomach after a horrible night of sleep. I spent the night thrashing around and when asleep, dreamt about a time when my life was worry free and nothing seemed like it could go wrong. The dreams all turned into nightmares. They all turned to the day that everything went wrong. When my cocky attitude put everything in jeopardy.

I realized that Chloe had already left and was on her way to Boston by the time I woke up. I had a day full of strategy meetings for my upcoming campaign planned and you would think that they would distract me from everything personal in my life but the entire day all I could think about was Chloe walking around the whole day with Trevor Cading. I didn't think she would recognize him but Trevor definitely knew who she was. Would Trevor tell her that he was Breanna husband? Surprisingly, that wasn't even my biggest fear. I knew that Chloe would be irate with me if she knew that I had known for the past five years that her sister had been married, but I could help her get over that.

My biggest fear was not knowing how much Trevor knew. What did he know about the past? What would he tell my wife? Chloe and I had drifted apart over the past five years but I couldn't lose her. People loved her; they loved the two of us as a couple. And she was a knockout. And even though I didn't always understand her, I did love her. She was my wife, my girl, and I was not going to let some asshole ruin everything for me. I would make sure that Trevor did not stand in my way of continuing my perfectly charmed life.

The day went on and as it started getting later I had to hold myself back from calling Chloe. She would call when she was on her way back as she had promised me. She never broke her promises to me; it was one thing I could always count on.

Around 4:00, when I didn't think I would be able to stand the suspense anymore, my phone rang. "Hello beautiful, are you just leaving? I was beginning to think I was going to have to send out a search party for you."

"So when were you planning on telling me about my brother-in-law Trevor Cading," Chloe asked in a sharp voice. I had never heard her sound so pissed.

"Baby, can we talk about this when you get home?" I asked in a gentle voice.

"You bet your ass we will," she said right before she hung up on me. I wasn't used to this. Before the accident Chloe used to get angry with me all of the time, but since then, she really didn't get angry. She would look sad from time to time but never this angry. I had gotten used to her listening to me and not yelling or talking back to me. I liked it that way. Most of my friends had wives who would argue with them all the time, sometimes even in public. They were all jealous of me whenever we had a late night out and they knew that they would be going home to be yelled at and I would walk through the door to a beautiful wife just smiling and not saying a word.

"Well shit," I said to myself. I had to fix this problem immediately. While Chloe has learned to control her feelings in front of the press and the public she was not as good at it as I was.

The press always seemed to capture photos where she was sad.

Especially right after the accident. It made for great headlines. Politician's wife: still dealing with issues from tragic attack. Although it made her a sympathetic person it was not the kind of press and exposure I was looking for. I needed the focus to be on my political views not her personal issues. I had to teach her to start controlling her facial expressions. She usually did a great job but she was not a politician and could not lie about her feelings as well as I could. I had a big event coming up and if she was still angry with me, someone in the press would figure it out. I made a quick decision, went to favorites on my phone and hit send with my fingers crossed that he could fix things.

"What can I do for you son," the judge's voice boomed.

"Dad, we have a problem, with Chloe," I said in a tense voice. As soon as Chloe and I had gotten married he had insisted on me calling him dad. My parents had been killed in a car crash when I was twelve and my grandpa had raised me but he had passed away from cancer three years before our marriage. Even though he was the closest thing I had to a father now I still hated calling the judge with a problem. Other than Chloe, he was the one person that I hated to disappoint. I couldn't very well spin a story to my wife and father-in-law the way I could to the press.

"What's the problem?" his voice got very serious and soft. "Is she ok," he asked with concern in his voice. One thing that I had in common with him was that Chloe was a main concern for both of us. We had done everything in our power to protect her and her mother from people and situations that we did not want them to be in.

"She went to visit some inner city schools today and Trevor Cading was the one who took her around. And he told her that he was Breanna's husband. I just got a call from her and she is very angry that I never told her about him. I wouldn't be surprised if she gave you a call later about it as well."

"Shit, what the hell was he doing showing her around?"

"I was stuck; that annoying lady who sat at our table set it up. I couldn't come up with a plausible reason why she shouldn't go without seeming suspicious."

"Ok, well then just tell her the truth." I winced a little. If only the judge knew the real reason why I didn't want Chloe to spend time with Trevor. What the hell did that damn cop know about the past?

"Just tell her that Breanna never told her mother and me about the wedding. While I found out later about the marriage, her mother never did. It would kill her mother if she knew. Tell her I asked you not to tell her about the marriage, because the fewer people who knew the better. You felt it would have been disrespectful to me to go against my wishes."

I breathed a sigh of relief. His reason completely made sense. I thanked him and said goodbye. After I hung up the phone I hurried home to get a romantic dinner ready. I would do everything in my power to keep Chloe from being angry with me, and more importantly, from being suspicious.

***

As I hung up the phone with Kevin I felt sick to my stomach. Although the plan I gave him definitely seemed plausible I could still feel the cold sweat forming on my head. I would not let Trevor ruin me and everything I had built. I went through too much trouble to keep my secret hidden. I had to make sure that Chloe didn't spend anymore time with him, ever again. As a judge I have seen a lot of scandal in my days in the courtroom. I've also seen what those scandals have done to the families. I would not let that happen to my family. My wife and daughter have been through enough. The truth would kill them both and destroy our family. I couldn't let anyone know about what I had done. I could not let them find out what had really happened. The truth of past had to stay where it belonged, in the past.

CHAPTER 6

I pulled in the driveway overflowing with a mix of emotions. I was beyond furious at Kevin and my father; I was excited at finding out more information about my past and about Breanna's past; and finally, I was thrilled that I recognized Trevor. Maybe this meant that I was beginning to remember. But surrounding this excitement and anger I was also very confused.

I definitely felt a strong attraction to Trevor. I had never felt this kind of attraction to anyone but Kevin before. And if I was being completely truthful with myself, I had never really felt that kind of pull and attraction to Kevin either. I mean I definitely found Kevin handsome; I would be an idiot if I didn't. I'd just never felt that feeling where your heart beats faster, your breath gets shorter and you feel it in your stomach. I shook my head disgusted with myself. I am sure when I first met Kevin I felt that way about him, I must have. I love Kevin even if he does act like a moron sometimes. I was just feeling this way because of the rut we had gotten ourselves into. But if the stories are all true, Kevin has always been my number one. If I weren't so furious at Kevin I would try to stay with him on the campaign trail.

Instead I was going to put all of my focus into figuring out why I went to Breanna and Trevor's house five years earlier.

I was hoping that Lily didn't know about Trevor. As sad as this confession is, I expect Kevin to do boneheaded things like this but a lie of omission this huge from Lily would definitely feel like a huge slap in the face and be difficult to forgive. I would find out later if Lily knew anything about this, but for now I had to deal with my jerk of a husband.

As I walked into my house I noticed that all of the lights were dimmed low and I could make out shadows from the flickering candle light in the dining room. I walked in to find Kevin waiting for me with a bottle of very expensive chardonnay chilling in the center of the table. There was also a wonderful aroma coming from the kitchen. Typically a romantic setting and his effort would warm me all over but not tonight. Did he really think that I would just forgive him because he cooked a meal, lit some candles and poured me a glass of wine?

"What is all this?" I asked keeping my voice low and cool. I was not going to give into him without hearing the reason he would keep such a huge thing a secret from me for so many years.

"Well, it's dinner. We need to eat and I figured we could talk over some great food and nice wine," he said, trying to sound reasonable.

I sat down across from him and waited for him while he put a plate in front of me with chicken cordon bleu, asparagus and zucchini bread. As he poured me a glass of wine I noticed that he was avoiding looking into my eyes.

"Well," I said once he sat down.

"Well, what?" he asked innocently.

“”Well what” I asked getting annoyed. “Well, why didn’t you tell me about Trevor? Tell me the truth because I am not in the mood for playing games right now,” I said, folding my arms against my chest completely ignoring the food and the wine.

“Baby,” he said with a sigh as he grabbed my hand and stroked it with his thumb. He finally glanced up at me, “Your mother never knew about the marriage. Your father asked me to keep it a secret. If your mom ever knew it would kill her. You know how sensitive your mother can be. She puts on a tough act but can you imagine finding out that your daughter not only didn’t invite you to the wedding but never even told you she was married,” he said with what I thought was a sincere look. “That would upset anyone.”

I tried to study his eyes. I felt like someone’s eyes told a lot about a person. If someone lied they would generally avoid eye contact. As I looked into his eyes I realized that he truly looked sincere. He did have a glimmer of desperation but I could not find anything that resembled deceit in his gaze. That didn’t mean that he wasn’t lying though. The problem with marrying a politician is that they are the best liars. I just couldn’t decide if I could trust him. I wanted to trust him which I told myself that it was simply because he was my husband, but to be truthful, I felt a little guilty for my unfaithful thoughts earlier in the day.

“Alright,” I said, releasing my hand from his. “I can understand not wanting to upset my mom and trying to protect her, but we are married. That means we have a partnership. You not telling me is the same as saying you don’t trust me. If you had told me the truth from the beginning and told me why my dad doesn’t want my mom to know I would have kept the secret, even if I don't agree with it. You don't have the right to not tell me such a huge thing when you know that I've been looking for answers for so long. I think my dad is wrong for not telling my mom and I'll tell him that but at the end of the day that is his cross to bear. How am I supposed to trust you when you don't trust me?

Kevin racked his hands through his hair and had a tortured look on his face as he tried to find the right words. "Listen there is no better way to put it, I fucked up and I'm truly sorry. I should have trusted you. You know that your parents are the closest things I have to parents and I felt I owed your father my silence. I was wrong," he said with eyes pleading for me to forgive him.

I sat shocked for a second, Kevin never, and I mean never, apologized for anything. "I'm still pissed but I do appreciate the apology. If you want me to forgive you though you can't keep secrets from me anymore. I need complete and total honesty."

"I can do that. I will do that," he said sincerely.

"Alright then," I said taking a bite of my dinner. One thing that Kevin had going for him was he was an excellent cook. I was decent but Kevin far surpasses me in the kitchen. If he wasn't such a ruthless politician I imagine he would of opened his own restaurant and be the head chef. Instead, when he wasn't running around from meetings to public appearances he treated cooking as a hobby and I got to experience all of his wonderful recipes.

"Alright," he said as a smile over took his face. Mixed with his smile I could almost detect some relief. "I'm sorry that you had to go through that shock today, when Trevor told you, it must have been overwhelming. I should have just told you before you went today, but again I didn't want to go against your father's wishes. His opinion just means so much to me and I hate to upset him. But I am so sorry I put you in a position to experience that kind of shock."

"It's ok," I said. "Well, actually no it wasn't ok but I know you were just trying to keep my father happy. You are right, though, it was extremely overwhelming. But I recognized him before he told me who he was. In fact the only reason he told me might have been because I recognized him."

"You recognized him," Kevin said in a shocked voice, whipping his gaze up from his plate to my face. "Your memory is coming back." He quickly set down his glass and stood up. "You should have called me right away when this happened, I am calling the doctor," he jumped up from his chair, knocking it backwards, and rushed over to the side table to grab his cell.

"Kevin no," I said almost yelling. "I didn't remember who he was; I just knew that I recognized him. My memories have not come back. If they really start fully come back we'll call the doctor. But not till then, I just don't want to feel false hope,"

"Of course, sweetheart," Kevin said slowly as he sat back down, turning his chair over and replacing his napkin in his lap. "I'm sorry I brought it up. It's just so exciting to think that you might recover your memory. You know that's what I've been hoping for throughout the past five years."

"I know it is," I said with a small pause before I asked him the real question I was just dying to know. "So I know I have asked you this a million times, so please don't be mad at me for bringing it up again. I just need to ask again. Why did I go to visit Breanna the night of the attack?" I asked slowly but earnestly.

Kevin looked shocked, "Baby you know I don't like to talk about that night, it just brings up bad memories."

"Kevin, complete honestly, remember you promised," I said with a tough edge to my voice.

"I know and I get it. Now that you know I have kept some things from you, you think I have kept other things from you too. I gotta tell you though, and I need you to believe me, that if I knew anything that might tell us who the killer is, I would have told you and the police immediately. I wouldn't keep something that huge from anyone. It's one thing to respect your father's wishes and not tell you about your sister's husband because it would break your mothers heart into a million pieces. It's another thing to allow a murderer to roam the streets," he said in a defensive voice coated in hurt.

"Kevin, I never said I think you wouldn't have gone straight to the police with any info about the killer. And I know that just because you made a mistake keeping some information from me doesn't mean I think you're a horrendous person. I know you don't know who killed Breanna but I wanted to know what you do know and anything that I might have said to you that day. What was my attitude? Was I upset, was I excited? How did I seem to you? I realize that it brings up bad memories but I need you to sort through those awful memories and help me. Do this for me, please," I said begging him once again.

Kevin studied my face for a moment and then set down his fork and sighed. "Sweetheart, that was five years ago. I wish I remembered everything but I don't remember that much about that day. The only thing I remember in detail is that horrible phone call I received telling me that you were in the hospital," Kevin said shaking his head at the memory.

"Kevin… please try," I said. "This is important to me."

He leaned back in his chair, closed his eyes, and then answered slowly. "Ok I'll do my best. I'll tell you everything I remember I just can't promise it'll provide any answers. I remember I'd been busy working all day. We were trying to find more money to go to the schools and the whole campaign team was on it. You, of course, were busy with your college classes. I talked to you once quickly in the afternoon. You were upset and agitated but you had a big test coming up so that was normal for you. You had such high expectations for yourself and you were always nervous that you would not keep your high GPA. Plus you were stressed because you thought we had chosen the wrong florist for the wedding. You never really mentioned Breanna very often back then. She would come up in conversation once in awhile but it was very rare. The last time I had heard you mention her you said that it was sad that you couldn't have her be a part of the wedding party. But you knew it would upset your parents, and again, your mom did not know about her marriage to Trevor."

"It is sad we weren't closer," I said mostly to myself.

"Sweetheart I am sorry that Trevor brought all of this up. I think it would be wise if you did not see him again. He'll just bring up issues that will only upset you. Plus what good is coming of this? You are just bringing up bad memories, and to be quite frank, this will just end up upsetting everyone."

"Kevin, I would think that you out of everyone would understand what good could come out of this. I could get my memory back and finally understand, not only the past, but who I am. You have no idea how it feels to have this big black hole in your life. It's so frustrating," I said, with tears filling up in my eyes. "Trevor and I are going to try to figure out what happened that night. I'll probably be seeing him at least once a week. And once we figure out what happened, and we will figure it out, I will probably continue to see him. He's my brother-in-law and regardless of what you and dad think, I think mom would agree with me and be happy that Breanna had found happiness."

Kevin did not try to disguise his disgust with the situation. "Chloe this is a bad idea. You're my wife and it's my duty to protect you and keep you away from people that could put you in harms way. I don't trust Trevor, I never have. He'll only give you false hope. The police searched for answers for years and were never able to find anything. I hate that Trevor is making you feel that you can find something that no one else has been able to discover. He's a cop. If he hasn't been able to find out any answers by now why would you believe that you two are going to find out what happened now?"

"Kevin, this is my decision, so please respect it. If we don't discover anything then I'll drop it and never bring it up again. But this is something that I need to do. I've never really looked for answers myself. I know you think it's your duty to protect me, but it's also your duty as my husband to support me, even if you may not agree with what I'm doing."

Kevin's face stayed hard. "Chloe I don't like this, but I'm also not going to try to stop you. If you need to do this, well then go ahead. But I'm not going to give you my blessing to spend time with Trevor. If you need to meet with Trevor then I'll come with you."

"That's very sweet, and thank you for the offer but you are so busy." As if to prove my point, his cell phone then rang.

"Kevin McDonald," he answered still scowling at me. He gave me one final disapproving look and then quickly left the room so he could take this call in private.

I finished my chardonnay and dinner alone, something I was very used to. I went upstairs, got undressed and got a steaming bath ready. One of my favorite parts of our house was the master bathroom. Its bathtub had Jacuzzi jets and was large and deep. It was the one feature of a house that I had begged for. The house initially did not have the tub so Kevin purchased it for me as a Christmas gift one year. As I soaked in the tub, feeling my tension slowly begin to ease away, I heard the handle for the bathroom open. Kevin came into the bathroom and lowered himself in the tub behind me. He whispered in my ear, "We'll figure out everything, but tonight let's just forget the day."

I slowly kissed Kevin and forgot about being angry with him. I was not a person who could stay mad at anyone for long. He picked me up and carried me into the bedroom. Twice in one week, this must be a record for us. As I fell asleep that night Kevin, my husband, did not fill my dreams. All night I dreamed about making love to my dead sister's husband, Trevor.

Chapter 7

It had been four days since I first met Chloe and I couldn't seem to get her out of my mind. I had snuck into the archives on Wednesday and made copies of all of the reports to give to her. If my captain caught me I knew he would have chewed me out, but it was worth it. I still had to be smart though and think this through: was it a stupid decision to drag her into this? I just couldn't move on with my life until I knew what happened that night. It has felt like my life had been frozen ever since Breanna died. With Chloe in the picture, though, I finally felt like a weight had been lifted off of my shoulders and there was a chance that I would get that closure I so desperately needed. Was it fair to her though?

One thing I didn't expect was the attraction I felt to Chloe. It was absurd and disrespectful to Breanna and I wanted to kick myself for it. But I couldn't help it. It was not only the attraction I felt for her but the intense sense of needing to protect her from any and everything. When I saw that punk kid hitting on her I wanted to rip him apart. If he weren't a kid I probably would have.

It appears that I am not the only person wanting to protect her though. On Wednesday I received two interesting phone calls. The first came from the high and mighty retired judge himself.

"Stay away from my family Trevor. Chloe doesn't need you," he said sternly with a growl in his voice. It was understandable why he intimidated so many people. I was not an average person though. Being a detective, I dealt with individuals trying to intimidate me on a regular basis. On top of that, I could frankly not give a damn what the judge wanted, or what he thought of me.

"Judge, I don't believe that's a decision for you to make. Against my better judgment, I respected your request to keep quiet about Breanna, but Chloe found out about me and she wants answers just as badly as I do. So sorry it bothers you but we'll be spending time together and there is nothing you can do about it." With that I hung up on him not waiting to hear his response. I am sure he was seething. In fact, there is a good chance I was the first person to ever hang up on him. For some reason that gave me a great deal of pleasure.

I received a similar call from the Governor. I responded the same way as I did to the Judge. The Governor informed me that he would be sending a bodyguard with Chloe when she came to visit me, which deeply amused me for some reason.

I had to laugh that they were all so threatened by me. I looked around my bare apartment and cracked open a beer, a very typical Saturday for me. I had tried to go on dates last year and found that I still wasn't ready. I really hadn't been even remotely emotionally, intellectually, or physically attracted to anyone since Breanna passed away. That is until I saw Chloe, which makes sense because she is Breanna's twin. As I turned on Saturday Night Live my cell rang. I didn't recognize the number and figured it was work related.

"This is Cading," I said abruptly.

"Hello Trevor," said the sweet voice of Chloe. My heart nearly stopped and I had to remind myself that this voice was not Breanna's.

"Hey Chloe. What can I do for you?" I said, trying to sound calm as my heart continued to pound at the voice that I almost mistook for my dead wife's.

"Well I've talked to a variety of my friends and to my family and I have a lot I want to talk to you about. The problem is that my husband can't stand the idea of the two of us meeting. He would like a bodyguard to escort me on Tuesday."

"If that's what you want, it's fine."

"Its not what I want though. What I want are answers and I would prefer to have both the questions and the answers stay between just you and me," she said simply.

"Alright, well what would you like me to do," I asked wondering where she was going with this.

"I was hoping we could meet before Tuesday. That way I can tell Kevin that we cancelled for Tuesday and I can pretend that I am busy doing something else when we do meet. I know he is leaving town tomorrow, so I was hoping we could meet then."

"That works for me, but I work until 7:00. So if you are alright with us meeting then, we could have dinner at my apartment and go over everything."

"Sounds great, I will see you then. I have to go now," she said.

"Chloe," I said softly.

"Yes?"

"Goodnight, have sweet dreams," I said unable to resist.

"Goodnight Trevor, have sweet dreams yourself."

We hung up the phones and I knew what I would be dreaming about that night.

***

"Are you almost done in there baby?" screamed Trevor through door.

I walked out of the bathroom with tears streaming down my face.

"Baby, what does it say?" Trevor said in a shaky voice.

I simply handed him the negative pregnancy test. I really thought I was pregnant this time.

"Shhhh, its ok love. We will have lots of babies eventually. It just wasn't the time," he said reassuring me.

He was right; we weren't even trying. He wiped my tears away and kissed my face. "I think right now would be a perfect time to try." He picked me up and carried me to the bedroom. He slowly kissed me. I could feel myself melting into him as he removed my tank top and pajama pants. The sadness I was feeling morphed into lustful desire for him. He began teasing me and I felt like every part of my body was going insane. I grabbed his hands and threw them above his head stopping him from conducting any more delicious torture. I became the one in charge and began to drive him crazy in every little way that I knew. When he could no longer take it he grabbed me and flipped on top of me. My body quivered as he entered into my body. He went very slowly back and forth inside of me. Every time I thought it could not get any better my body started to go even crazier. He continued to kiss me softly on my lips to my neck to my nipples. My body was just about to convulse in an orgasm when I heard a loud beeping noise. What was that noise? Make it stop!

I quickly sat up in my bed breathing hard. "Shhh baby, go back to sleep, you don't need to get up yet," Kevin said. I have to get ready for my flight. I'll see you when I get back." He kissed me on the check as I slowly laid back down and then he hopped out of the bed.

It was only dream. But it seemed so real. I needed to get control of myself this was getting out of hand.

Chapter 8

"Annabelle, what a pleasant surprise running into you like this," Mrs. Patterson said with an extremely fake smile as I got into the checkout line behind her. I gave her an equally fake "what the hell do you want" smile back, not even bothering to say hi.

"Well, please tell your family I said hello and we really should all grab dinner some time," she said, grabbing her bags and scooting away from me like I had the plague. I couldn't even grocery shop in peace without someone sticking up their self-righteous nose at me. It's almost comical to picture her and the judge having dinner with my family. They couldn't stand us almost as much as I couldn't stand them,

This just brought back the memory from earlier in the day. I couldn't believe those bitches from *The Ladies of Cape Cod* would not let me be part of their group. I didn't come from the richest family but I went to school with all of them and my best friend growing up was Breanna Patterson. Her sister Chloe was one ringleaders of their ridiculous little group. Granted Breanna and I had a huge falling out. I really don't know how we were ever friends in the first place. It was one of those situations that we had just been friends for so long that we just continued the friendship in high school.

During our senior year the friendship began to fade but we were still there for each other until the midterm for our calculus class. We sat next to each other and I was having a rough time with the class. Breanna was flying through it without a problem as she did with most of her classes. I knew I had to do well on the test or I would risk ruining my GPA. Breanna studied with me all week and she gave me the confidence to think I would do great on the test.

The second the midterm was placed on my desk my mind went completely blank. I couldn't remember one single equation. So I did the only thing I could think of, I glanced over at Breanna's test and copied hers. Unfortunately, Mrs. Hauhn saw me copying Breanna's test. She threatened to expel us both and we ended up with zeroes on the test. Breanna refused to speak to me after that, like it really mattered to her. Her daddy could have gotten her into whatever school she wanted to go to. I ended up having to forfeit my dream of going to an Ivy League school and had to settle on UMass. It was still a decent school but definitely not Harvard like I had planned. It was ironic that the test really didn't matter at all to Breanna since she ran away and I doubt she ever even went to college.

Breanna had in some ways ruined me though. She made it known that I had copied her test and that we were no longer friends. She was never popular in high school but Chloe had her back and once Chloe said I was a bitch it spread like wildfire. No one crossed Chloe in high school. If she didn't like someone then everyone didn't like that person. My senior year of high school ended up being one of the worst years in my life. I realize that it was a long time ago but still, to this day, those snooty girls stick their noses up at me and act like they are way above me. I will never forgive the Patterson twins for all they did to me. No matter how much time passed the hate I felt for the both of them never seemed to fade, if anything it seemed to grow in leaps and bounds every year.

I had to smile to myself though at the final revenge I took on the twins. They had never seen it coming. It's just a shame that Chloe has no memory of everything that happened, maybe one day I'll have to change that. But for now I will just enjoy in the bliss of knowing that I brought down the great Breanna Patterson.

***

I hurried to my car after grabbing my groceries. Ever since Breanna left town Annabelle has given me the creeps. That may seem horrible since she is so young but there was just something always off about her. She practically lived at my house as a child but something changed between her and Breanna and she just got nasty.

It wasn't until a year after Breanna left that I actually found out what happened. Chloe told me one day. I was absolutely furious that the school never told me about the incident and then to find out they had told my husband – as usual he had wanted to protect me from being upset and protect Breanna from being in trouble. I should have yelled and screamed at him, but instead I said nothing and went about my normal day.

Reflecting on anything that happened back then was always upsetting. It was just such an ugly past; one I wish I could just overlook. I couldn't let it go though. Forgetting the past would mean I would be forgetting Breanna. I wish I could go back in time and change things but unfortunately that's not an option.

I remember the day the twins were born. It was the happiest day of my life. I recall thinking my heart would explode from the amount of love I had for them. I vowed, that day, to be the best mother any woman could possibly be. I had broken that promise though. I had not acted in the best interest of my girls and I had not protected them from the horrors of the world. In fact, I did the exact opposite. I did a horrible thing. What I did, no mother should ever be forgiven for. I know I will never forgive myself. The only thing I could do was try to forget, and try to make everyone else forget.

If my husband wanted to protect me from reliving the past, I would let him to do it. If only he knew what he was protecting me from.

Chapter 9

I woke up early on Sunday and decided that if Trevor and I were meeting that night then I should spend the day playing detective Chloe. I quickly showered and grabbed some coffee as I headed toward the door determined to come up with some new information.

Before I went out the door I picked up my cell phone and gave Lily a call. I had been avoiding her calls, afraid to ask her if she knew about Trevor. It was time to stop being a wuss though and find out what she knew.

The phone only rang twice before she answered, "Chloe McDonald where the heck have you been? I was getting ready to send a search party out for you! I was having a major crisis yesterday, nothing looked good on me! I needed to raid your closet!"

"Sorry Lil, I had a lot on my mind and I needed time to think. Ok, I need to ask you a question and I need you to be completely honest with me," I rambled on with my fingers crossed and my heart pounding through my chest. I guess I was even more nervous for this conversation then I realized.

"Ok," she said her voice getting much more serious. "Is everything ok?"

"It will be. I think I am finally going to start to get some answers to everything I've been searching for, but first I need to know if you knew about Trevor?"

"Trevor, Trevor who?" she asked sounding honestly confused.

I took a deep breath calming myself down. "Trevor Cading, my sister's husband."

"What!" Lily screamed in my ear, which brought a smile to my face and officially stopped my heart from pounding. She didn't know! "Breanna was married! What, when, where… what the hell! How did we not know about this? How the hell do you know about this now?"

I laughed. It felt good to feel the nervous knot in my stomach go away and my heart calm down. "I know, I was as shocked as you when I found out. I apparently knew, but I don't know how long I knew before the accident."

"Wait you knew and didn't tell me?" She said sounding genuinely hurt. This was a change. I hadn't expected to hurt her feelings.

"I am sorry Lil, but for all I know I found out right before the accident. I'm not sure about the details."

"Ok, that is fair," she said after a moment. "I obviously can't be mad at you for something you can't even remember. Plus, you know how I hate being mad at you. So, moving on, what are you doing now?"

"I'm about to head out and start talking to people. Trevor and I decided we are going to search for answers. Which means I need to start with you and ask you questions."

"OK," she said sounding unsure. "I have a million questions for you too starting with how did you meet Trevor, but we can touch on all of that at a different time. All right, if answers are what you need I'll do anything to help you. Shoot, I'll help as much as I can. I know I've been hesitant in the past but that isn't fair to you. You deserve to know as much as possible."

My heart warmed for my best friend. I could always count on her. I felt badly for having doubted her at all. "Is there anything you can tell me about the day or week of the attack that would help me? Is there anything that I should know? Think beyond what you have told me in the past, think about little things that may have not seemed like a big deal at the time, but could possibly be a clue to something else." I realized I was rambling. "I'm sorry, I know I am not making complete sense."

"No, you make complete sense. I just need a second to think." Lily was then quiet for a moment, "I have thought about this for along time," she said quietly. "Now I don't know anything for sure. The only thing I know is that I talked to you that day and you didn't tell me where you were going. To be honest, I was trying to talk to you about some stupid boy problem I was having. You told me you couldn't talk, you said you had stuff you had to deal with. The weird thing is I mentioned something about boys sucking before we got off the phone and you said yea boys suck and so does Annabelle. I asked you what you were talking about but you said you had to run and that you'd tell me later. I never got a chance to ask you again what you were talking about." She stopped for a second, "I'm sorry Chloe."

"Lil no! This is so helpful! This gives me a place to start! I love you bunches, thank you for being the best friend ever."

We got off the phone and I quickly grabbed my purse and headed out to my car. My first stop was Annabelle's office. I kept my fingers crossed that she had time to meet with me and hoped she wouldn't be too annoyed that I hadn't made an appointment first. After talking to Lily I needed to know why I had been mad at her. I realized it might have been nothing, but even without my memories something in my gut has always told me that I had a reason to not like Annabelle. There has to be a reason for that. Even if I had to push my way into her office, it was time I know why she has always made me uncomfortable and why I've never liked her.

After graduating from college Annabelle now worked for a local law firm. She specialized in divorces, although apparently she was not very good. If the rumors around town were true, then the only reason she hasn't been fired yet is because she knows how to give special treatment to her boss and to a variety of clients.

The receptionist took my name and called Annabelle's office. "She can see you now," the receptionist said pointing to the door with Annabelle's name on it. "You can let yourself in."

I opened the door and there she sat. She was a very pretty woman in a sleazy kind of way. She wore way too much makeup on her pale skin, her fiery red hair hung down around her shoulders, and her outfit was definitely not appropriate for a work setting. Her blouse was unbuttoned way to low and she had on a very short black skirt topped off with stilettos, definitely not practical for the courtroom.

"Chloe, what an unexpected surprise," she said with a fake friendliness to her voice.

"Thanks for agreeing to see me with no notice," I said trying hard to be as pleasant as possible sitting in a chair across from her desk and giving her an equally fake smile in return. "I need your help with something that is very important to me."

"Don't tell me you and Kevin are getting a divorce!" Annabelle said in a shocked voice. "Not Cape Cod's all star couple!"

"No, no, nothing like that," I said quickly cutting her off. "I have decided that it is time that I do some investigating of my own about Breanna's death. So I decided to talk to the people that were closest to her."

Annabelle's face did not hide her surprise. "Why now? Why after five years?"

"I recently met someone who made me realize that I don't really know anything about my sister's life after she left, and it made me realize that if I can learn more about her life, and my own life for that matter, I might be able to piece together what happened."

"Well I don't know how much I'm going to be able to help you. My friendship with Breanna ended way before she died."

"Why did it end?"

She took a slow breath and studied me before answering. "Well it's simple. She turned her back on me as a friend, decided that she was better than me. She just had everyone fooled, everyone thought she was a sweet, decent person and in reality she was just the same as everyone else. She sat on her pedestal and looked down on the rest of us. Our friendship ended abruptly and a couple of months later she left town. That was the last I heard of her and I had no desire to talk to her again."

"Do you have any idea why she left town?"

"Why would I know?" she sneered. "It might shock you but after she was an absolute bitch to me I didn't spend time paying attention to what you and your dead sister did."

I breathed in a sharp breath at her callous remark. "I understand you two had your fallout but how can you be so cruel? She was your best friend for years and while I understand we weren't close I am sure we had some sort of relationship. Right?"

"You are kidding me, right? You were an absolutely horrendous bitch to me and I have no reason to be nice or step on tip toes around you."

"I am sorry to hear that," I said genuinely. "If I hurt you in the past I apologize. But that isn't me now and from what I understand Breanna was always kind and fair to everyone."

"Have you not been listening to me?" Annabelle then raised her voice to a yell. "Breanna wanted everyone to think she was so great and so perfect but she was a backstabbing fuckin bitch! So don't sit there and act like you know anything about her because news flash you don't. Whoever the lucky SOB who took out Breanna and gave you the whack you deserved took away your memories of that fake sister of yours!"

"Enough!" I screamed back. I was beyond shocked at all the horrendous things coming out of Annabelle's mouth. How can someone be so awful? "How dare you! I am so sorry you didn't get to enact your revenge on me and my sister!" I said in a voice dripping in sarcasm. "But seriously what is wrong with you?"

She gave a twisted smile and sat back down in her chair and lowered her voice. "Don't worry, let's just say I got some revenge of my own."

"What do you mean?" I asked lowering my voice to a soft whisper a little nervous to hear her answer.

"I just remembered that I do know why Breanna left town but unfortunately for you, that is one thing that you will never know. I made a pact with someone and have no desire to break it. Especially not for you."

***

After Chloe left my office I sat there for a second, kicking myself for possibly divulging too much information. I couldn't help it though. It was too wonderful to see the shocked, confused look on her face. She would probably run back to her posse of skanks and tell them how horrible I am but what could they possibly do to me now? They already look down on me, well now maybe they will know that I am not one to be messed with. The only thing that left a nervous pit in my stomach was wondering how he'll react when he hears what I told Chloe. He is the only person I never want to upset. He is the one person that truly gets me. Hopefully he understands. One thing is for sure, as I told Chloe, I will never give up our secret. I made a promise to him years ago and I will take that secret to my grave. I love him and will do anything to keep him happy.

***

I quickly escorted myself out of Annabelle's office. She refused to answer any more questions about what she said claiming she had to prepare for a meeting. I walked out to my car with my head spinning and my thoughts a jumbled mess. What the hell did she do? How could she have made

Breanna leave town? How is this the first time anyone has heard anything about this? What the hell is going on? She seemed busting at the seams to let me know that she was responsible for Breanna fleeing town. Granted, that was after she got heated and upset. Has she been waiting all this time to tell someone her secret? How has no one asked her about anything before this? Although I had to remind myself that many people have shielded me from the truth before so maybe she has blabbed to other people. My mind just kept flooding with more questions, none that I had answers to, just questions that brought up other questions. My phone ringing broke my stream of thought.

"Hey mom, what's up?"

"Ugh, I'm so stressed. I think I am going to need to fire my trainer. I was just told by someone that my arms were looking bulky. Bulky! Can you believe it! I want to look toned, not bulky!"

"Mom, you look fine. You have nothing to worry about."

"Thanks sweetie," she said with stress still in her voice. "How's your day going? Sad Kevin is out of town?"

"My day has certainly been interesting," I said slowly trying to decide if I wanted to open this can of worms with my mother. I decided that if I'm really committed to finding out answers I can't leave anyone out of my questioning. "Mom, did Breanna ever talk to you about why she and Annabelle had a falling out?"

"What makes you think that they had a falling out?" she said her voice turning serious.

"Because Annabelle told me that they did. She also told me that Breanna left town because of something she did."

"What?" my mom said shocked. "Did she tell you what it is that she did?"

"No, she wouldn't give me any details."

"That little witch. I never did like her. I am going to be honest with you, I knew that they had a falling out, but the idea that she did something that made Breanna leave town just seems preposterous. Their falling out how to do with Annabelle cheating off of Breanna on a test. That is not a reason that Breanna would leave town. She probably made that whole story up just to mess with your head."

"You really think so?" I asked. I hadn't even thought of that possibility. But my mom was right; Breanna wouldn't run away because she was angry with Annabelle for cheating off of her on a test. After hearing how nasty she was in the office it is possible that she wanted to mess with my head. Anything was possible. It was also possible she had done something additional to Breanna and that Annabelle told me about it the day I went to see Breanna and that is why I was pissed at her years ago.

"I definitely think so. What brought up this conversation between you and Annabelle?"

"I asked her. Mom, its time I found out what happened five years ago."

"Chloe, we have been down this path a million times before. We have sat looking at photos; we've gone to countless therapists. It isn't like we haven't tried before. I don't know why you think this time will be different than any other time. Don't you think it's time for us to let the past rest and to move forward with our lives?"

"Mom, I understand what you are saying and I know you're right. You just don't know what its like to have this hole in my life. It is so important to me to find answers."

"Chloe, No one understands wanting to find out what happened more then me. The attack was the single most devastating thing that has ever happened in my life. No mother should bury their child." She said her voice shaking.

"I am so sorry, I didn't mean to upset you. I promise I won't bring it up to you again. But I am going to continue to search for answers."

"Chloe, this is your choice, but please be careful. I have already lost one child and I don't want to watch my remaining child have her heart broken."

I hung up the phone and thought about what she said. I wasn't searching for answers to hurt the people I loved. Just the opposite, I want to find closure not only for myself, but also for my parents and for Trevor.

I decided to grab a bite to eat and then head home for a short nap. I didn't want to drive through rush hour traffic so I wanted to be on the road by 3:00. I figured I could talk to a few people in Boston before I met up with Trevor.

I laid down for my nap and tried to make a mental list of the people I wanted to speak to both in Cape Cod and in Boston.

***

"Listen sis, I need you to come to Boston today. I need to talk to you. I've been a terrible sister and I should have talked to you a long time ago. There is so much stuff that you need to know. Life is not as perfect as you think it is. I learned the hard way, and you shouldn't have to discover all of this awful crap like I did. Please come here and let me tell you the truth about everything."

I woke up with my heart beating out of my chest. Is it possible? Did I just have a memory? It was like I was watching a movie. I could see Breanna talking on the phone, standing in her foyer. I felt like I was the one talking on the phone, yet I also felt like I was on the other end of the phone listening. If it was a memory I would have only been on one end of the phone. So was this a memory or was it just my mind's way of making up memories to answer some of my own questions.

I quickly got dressed and headed out to go meet the real detective who may have some answers of his own.

Chapter 10

"Do you think he could have done it?" asked my partner, Detective Robb Brown.

Robb had been my partner for what seemed like forever. We worked perfectly together. We seemed to complement each other just right. In our department we had the highest number of solved cases. When everything had happened with Breanna he was one of the people who helped me keep it together. I confided in him that even though I was told to stay far away from the case I couldn't do it. He knew that I was doing my own investigating and he could have easily reported me to the captain. Instead of turning me in, though, he helped me. Unfortunately, we were unable to find out anything and he ended up being the one punished. Everyone felt sorry for me and understood why I was trying to investigate but they said he should have had enough common sense to know better. He ended up getting put on a desk for three months. Just for helping me out. That's why I made the decision to work the cases we are assigned and keep him in the dark about everything going on with Chloe.

I shook my head and tried to get my mind back on track. This case deserved just as much dedication as I was giving my wife's case. A third grade teacher had been shot and her family needed answers just as much as I did. We suspected her husband was our perp. She had a boy toy on the side and we believed that her husband had just found out about his wife's infidelities.

"I think it is time we get a warrant to get in that house. We won't get one tonight though; we will have to try for one in the morning."

"Sounds good to me. If that's the case I'm gonna call it. All of the guys are going out to Martinis tonight if you want to meet us up there."

"Thanks, but no thanks. I already have plans. But you guys have fun."

His eyebrow raised a little, "What kind of plans? You got a date? You getting back in the game?

I had to laugh. I should have guessed he wouldn't have left it with a simple I have plans. I never miss a night at Martinis. It was always a fun time out, plus the owner was a retired cop and gave us great deals. "Don't get too excited, nothing like that. I'm trying out a new trainer and he wasn't available this morning. So while you are getting blasted with the guys I will be getting my ass kicked at the gym." I hated lying to him but if I told him the truth he would demand to help and that only meant trouble for him.

Alright brotha, see you later."

"Night." After Robb left I finished up some paperwork and got the warrant request ready. As I put on my jacket my thoughts went immediately back to Chloe. I couldn't help but wonder if she had any new information, but it was more than that. I was just looking forward to seeing her. It had been a long time since I had been excited to see someone. It was just a shame that I never spent time with Chloe when Breanna was alive. I couldn't help but feel like if we had known each other in the past this would be way less awkward.

I grabbed my cell phone out of my pocket. The phone rang a few times before her voice answered, "hello".

"Hey Chloe, it's me. I was just wondering how far from Boston you were."

"Oh I'm actually already here. I left earlier this afternoon. I wanted a chance to look into a few things here."

"Well I'm leaving the station right now, so why don't you meet me at my place. We can order some takeout once I get there."

"Sounds great. I will see you there."

I hurried home to made sure not to make her wait. As I pulled into the driveway of my apartment building I saw that Chloe had in fact had beat me there. As she got out of her Lexus I studied her. She looked absolutely breathtaking. For the millionth time I had to remind myself that she was my sister in law and not Breanna.

"Welcome to my humble home," I said opening the door for her. We walked into my apartment, which happens to be on the first floor, and Chloe got settled on the couch. I quickly ordered some Chinese takeout. "So, tell me what you learned today."

Chloe quickly recounted her talk with Lily, her visit with Annabelle, her conversation with her mother and her dream. "After I got to Boston I met up with Bill Martin. I really didn't learn anything from him accept that he's a dirt bag."

I winced. Bill was Breanna's old boss and he was a true jerk. I had forced Breanna to quit that job because of the way he treated her. After she had officially quit I had a confrontation with him about that way he regarded my wife and women in general. I hated the idea of Chloe dealing with him. "It sounds like you found out some good info, especially from Lily and Annabelle, and if you are right and that was a memory then you're definitely on the right track. I think from now on though you should focus your energy on the people in Cape Cod and if you want to talk to someone in Boston let me know and I can come with you."

"Sounds good to me," she said lightly. She picked up the copy of the case report that I had placed on the coffee table. She started to read it intensely, as she was reading the report she began to rub her shoulder and winced.

"Knot?" I asked.

"Yea it's not a big deal, I think I just slept on it wrong when I was napping today."

"Here maybe I can help," I said sitting on the couch next to her. She hesitated and then turned her back to me continuing to read the report. I started to rub her back and realized that she not only had knots but also was extremely tensed. I focused my energy on loosening her back up and heard a sigh escape from her lips.

"This feels amazing," she said.

After I finished up with her back I noticed that her face had turned to confusion and worry. "The report all seems normal. But there is one thing that I don't understand," she said.

"What's that? I asked moving even closer to her trying to see what she was reading.

"Well, it says that Breanna was shot in the chest."

"Yea what is weird about that?"

"Well if you turn to the medical report, it states that she died due to a gun shot to her small intestine."

I realized what she was getting at. "How did I miss this," I said mostly to myself. "Why would the police put that she was shot in the chest when she was clearly shot in her stomach?"

"It could just be a simple mistake but it just seems odd."

"That's a big mistake for a homicide detective to make. I will have words with him tomorrow."

With that the doorbell rang. "Food is here," I quickly jumped to my feet, grabbed my wallet and got the food from the delivery boy.

While we ate our Chinese our conversation turned to lighter subjects. "I am telling you the truth," she said laughing so hard that tears were running down her face. "I actually had to walk through a bank drive thru! I needed to deposit some money, the ATM was down and my car was in the shop! I didn't even think to call a cab!" she said now holding her side because she was still laughing hysterically.

I couldn't help but to start cracking up. "You know I have not had this much fun in a long time," I said still laughing.

She calmed down and looked me dead in the eyes and lowered her voice to a whisper, "me either".

With that, not even thinking I leaned forward grabbed the back of her head and kissed her. Thoughts of Breanna slipped into my mind as I kissed her harder. It felt like time had reversed itself and nothing had ever changed. I felt her lips part to mine and heard her give a soft sigh. I moved closer and whispered, "Breanna".

I felt her whole body immediately go rigid and she quickly away from me. Before I knew it she was on her feet and picking up her purse.

"It's getting really late, I mean I should probably head out now," she quickly stammered as she headed to the door.

"Chloe, wait! I'm so sorry; I got caught up in the moment and..."

She quickly waived me off with her hand. "Listen this was as much my fault as it was yours so how about we forget this little incident ever happened and just go back to our investigation, shall we?" she said with a little smile.

"Yea I think that is a good idea," I said now walking with her to the door. "And again Chloe," I said turning her to look at me. "I'm sorry."

"So am I," she said with a small smile and a face that held a sad and confused expression. She walked out the door and I wondered if my face held the same expression.

***

"You can never tell mommy and daddy about this!"

"I won't Chloe! Show me!" I said exasperated! Chloe always found the coolest things. I sometimes would get so mad at her but she always ended up sharing with me so it was hard to stay mad.

Chloe slowly inched Daddy's office door open, peeking in to make sure no one was in there. "Ok come on," she urged me forward into the room. Once I was inside the room she quickly shut the study door and hurried over to the bookcase.

"Ok, you ready," she said with a mischievous smile.

"Yes!" I nearly screamed as I felt the excitement bubble up inside of me.

"Ok here it is!" With that she pushed on the middle bookcase. At first not much happened and then it begin to give beneath her tiny weight. As she pushed the bookcase a room began to appear behind it.

"A hidden room!" I gasped with my eyes widened in amazement.

Chloe smiled and pulled me inside the room and quickly closed the bookcase so we were shut inside the room. "This will be our secret room," she said in a whisper. "Whenever one of us is sad or needs sometime away from mommy and daddy we can come here and no one will be able to find us! We will be the only ones that know about this room. And look," she said pointing to something I could not make out in the dark room.

"I can't see, it's too dark," I whispered back.

She quickly turned on the flashlight we took from the kitchen. The light shined and I immediately took in the room. It was nothing fancy, not like our pretty pink matching bedrooms. It was just a plain room, very small with one chair and a table in the corner. It was not much of anything. Chloe was right though; it was incredible for the fact that it was all ours. No one would know about it but us and we would always have our special place. "How did you find this, sis?"

"On accident! I was just playing around with daddy's books and I tried to push one of his books back into place and the bookcase budged! I couldn't believe it and I know that daddy doesn't know. He doesn't even read any of these books; he just has them here to look smart. I overheard him tell one of this friends that!"

I smiled, Chloe overhears everything. I was so lucky to have her as my sister and as my best friend. I don't know what I would do without her. All the kids always liked her but she always stood up for me and told everyone they had to be nice to me. I don't know what I would do without her!

"Breanna look though!" Chloe said impatiently. She was shining the flashlight on what appeared to be a black circle that was hanging on the wall. She slowly moved the black circle and it revealed a hole. "A peep hole," she said confirming my suspicion. It goes through to the study, we can hear and see everything that happens in there and mommy and daddy will never know we are here!"

I laughed, but on cue daddy walked into the office. He shuffled around his desk and picked up his phone. He made what sounded like a very important phone call. Daddy has the greatest job in the world! He makes sure that bad people go to jail and that they don't hurt any more people. I couldn't think of anyone else who had a more important job.

As he left the room Chloe opened up the door and we eased out of our secret room. "Remember, Bre, this is very important! We cannot tell anyone about this. This is our room and our room only."

As she stuck out her pinky for me I grabbed it with my pinky and whispered, "I promise."

***

I woke up with a jolt. Siting up I tried to figure out what had woken me from my sleep; and almost on cue a huge crash of thunder shook the house. That explains that I thought. I looked at my clock and saw that it said 3:30. I had only fallen asleep a few hours earlier. After my eventful night with Trevor I had a hard time falling asleep. I could not believe I had been unfaithful to my husband. Not only was I unfaithful to my husband but with my dead twin sister's husband. How sick is that! If someone pitched my story to Dr. Phil he would have me on the show in no time ready to analyze my sick and twisted mind. I knew I wasn't going to fall back to sleep so I led myself downstairs to the kitchen and poured myself a glass of milk. It wasn't until I was sitting on the kitchen stool and had my milk and chocolate chip cookie in front of me that my thoughts shifted from my tonight's events to my dream.

Again the dream felt so real, like a memory. It is funny how when I dream I am Breanna, it was my way of trying to remember my sister. One aspect that made me feel good is that I can easily find out if this was just a dream or some kind of memory. My parents still lived in the same house and I could simply find out if the "secret room" that I dreamt about exists. My guess was the room does not exist, but I would never know until I went over there and tried to shove the bookcase to make the room appear.

I took out my cell phone and without thinking dialed one of the last numbers that popped up on my caller ID.

"Hello," said a very groggy voice.

"I am so sorry to be calling this late," I said immediately regretting the phone call I just placed.

"Chloe," said Trevor, his voice turning from groggy to very alert. "What time is it? Are you ok?"

"I'm fine," I said quickly to reassure him. "I'm just having trouble sleeping and I was thinking about our investigation.

I just wanted to make sure that you're going to talk to the individual who wrote up the police report."

"Of course I will and I'll let you know what he has to say about the report after I talk to him." He paused for a second then went on. "Why don't you tell me why you are having trouble sleeping, is it because of me and everything that happened tonight?" He questioned sounding very guilty.

"Actually no, I just…" I was about to tell him about my dream and decided that it was silly. "It is nothing, go back to sleep I'm sorry I woke you, goodnight," I quickly hung up the phone before he could even respond. I shook my head at myself. What was the point of that? I think I just wanted to hear someone's voice and wanted to talk to someone.

The person I should be calling is Kevin, my husband. I was about to pick up the phone and dial him and realized how angry he would be at me for waking him. I decided against it and closed my phone. What would I say to him anyways? Hey honey, I am calling to tell you I kissed my dead sister's husband, oh and then I had a dream and in the dream I was her. I headed upstairs shaking my head at myself and laid back down into bed knowing that I was just going to be lying there waiting until it was an appropriate time to get up and start my day.

Chapter 11

"Baby, I'm going to be later than I expected," I said into the phone while covering my other ear to block out the annoying screeching child in the background. "My flight was delayed due to maintenance issues with the plane."

"It's ok, take a deep breath, a delayed flight is nothing to get all upset over," Chloe said in her soothing voice. The level of my annoyance was evidently coming through over the phone. There was nothing I hated more than dealing with things I couldn't control. I had a million things to do and the last thing I needed was to have my schedule interrupted. I took a deep breath and decided to switch topics. "So what have you been up to, anything new?"

Chloe took a deep pause. I could feel my stomach tighten. "No, nothing worth mentioning," she said softly and quickly. "So I was thinking we should try out Tom's new Italian restaurant when you get home," she said switching the topic a little too quickly for my liking.

The rest of the conversation was pretty typical. I could tell that she was leaving something out, though. It wasn't like Chloe to keep anything from me. I may have my share of secrets and small deceptions, but Chloe was always honest and up front. As I spoke with her the wheels in my head began to turn. I realized it was time to call on my friend, Ethan. Ethan and I went all the way back to our childhoods. He was someone that I could trust, someone who minded his own business and most importantly someone who knew how to keep secrets. His job depended on his discretion. Yes, I thought to myself. It is definitely time to call on Ethan.

***

"Susan will you please pass me the salt," I said while reading the front page of the paper.

"No," she said simply as she continued to read her book. I gave a sharp glance up and scowled at her. Her face had a nice cool smile and she lifted her eyes to me. With humor in them she said," the doctor says you have to cut down on your sodium intake, remember?"

I mumbled some kind of disgruntled reply to her as I looked back down at my paper. As I was trying to think of some reason why I should get to have salt for my eggs the doorbell cut through the silence. "Who could that be," I wondered out loud. As I opened the door I couldn't help but feel surprised when I saw who our visitor was. "Chloe! What brings you here so early?

"Hey dad," she said quickly kissing my cheek and walking into the front foyer. "Sorry for the early intrusion but I have a busy day today and I think I dropped my favorite lipstick in your office when I was here last week."

"I haven't seen it but feel free to go look for yourself."

"Thanks dad!" she said breezing past me and walking towards the office. I studied my daughter and realized for the millionth time how important she was to me. She was a huge part of my life. She and Susan were my life. I was not going to let anyone ruin that. If that meant I had to find other means to get rid of Trevor Cading then so be it. I was willing to stop at nothing to make sure that nothing disrupted my family again.

***

I walked into the so familiar office and looked to the spot I saw in my dream. Quietly closing the door behind me I hurried over the place that seemed so familiar but also so far in the back of my mind at the same time. As I touched the same spot that I had in my dream, and sure enough, the secret room of my dream opened to me. I gasped in shock, was it actually possible that my memories were coming back to me? I walked into the room hoping that more memories would flood back but nothing. I just stared at the room that my sister and I had shared when we were children. The only thing I could figure is that somehow my subconscious brought back the memory of the room and I had that dream. For what reason I have no idea, but then again it was just a dream. I have had a ton of dreams over the years and most of them have meant nothing. There is no reason that this one should be any different.

***

"Trevor, snap out of it! What do you think of this?" my partner said referring to our current case.

"Oh yea, sorry" I said taking my reading glasses off and rubbing my temples. "I think that the man is sketchy as hell and I think we need to pressure him and start making his life a fuckin nightmare to get a confession out of him," I said, switching my thoughts back to the murder case in front of me. It was hard to stay focused when there was only one case I wanted to investigate. I kept going over new details. I now need to have another conversation with the detective who handled the case as well as the medical examiner to figure out what happened with the case report. It could have been just a simple mistake but my gut was telling me something was off and one thing I have learned over the years is to always trust my instincts. I also couldn't help but think about Annabelle and what Chloe told me about their conversation. From what Breanna used to tell me about her, when she would mention her, she was quite the sleaze, which made me think maybe I could get some additional information out of her that Chloe was not able to obtain. At that moment I decided it was time I make my own trip to Cape Cod. "Listen man, I need to head out," I said grabbing my coat and running out the door. "I am sorry to leave you hanging but you will do great on this case. I'm not able to focus right now. I have another case that needs my full attention at the moment." I ran out as I heard Robb yelling protests and probably wondering why I was on another case without him.

As I pulled onto Cape Cod I decided to go straight to the Parker and Parker Law Firm to speak with Annabelle. As I was driving into p-town I couldn't help but notice that a car that seemed to be tailing me. I decided to make a few turns to see if I could lose the car, sure enough though the car was still right behind me. Making a mental note of the make and model of the car I continued on.

Before I went into the law firm, though, I realized that if I expected Chloe to let me know when she came to Boston I should do her the same courtesy and give her a call to let her know that I was on the Cape. As I pulled into a parking spot in front of the law firm I picked up my cell and hit Chloe's name from my call log. It only rang a couple times before an abrupt hello answered on the other end. Chloe's light airy voice that I was expecting was replaced by an angry deep male voice. "Governor I was hoping to speak to your wife," I said irritated.

"She's busy, if you would like to leave her a message you can, but be assured I will throw it away," he hissed. "Please do not call back," he said slamming down the phone not giving me a chance to respond.

"Wonderful," I mumbled to myself. I didn't mean to get Chloe in trouble with that prick. Breanna would not even let us talk about him when she was alive. That showed me how much she hated him. In addition, anytime he would pop on TV she would whisper jerk under her breath and change the channel. If she ever swore I'm sure the word would have been a lot stronger. Her hatred of him formed my initial feelings towards him, then following Bre's death my feelings grew stronger. I am pretty sure I hate him more now than Breanna ever did.

I remember how I used to ask Breanna why she disliked Kevin, "If your sister loves him then there must be something good about him," I used to say to her. She always had the same response, "That's just because Chloe doesn't know the real Kevin." I would push her to try to understand what she meant but she never wanted to go into it. Now that she is gone and I have gotten to know her sister

I wished more than ever that I knew what Breanna knew about Chloe's husband. I had a gut feeling that she needed to be protected from him but I had nothing but my instincts to prove it. Well, maybe Annabelle could shine some light on that subject I thought as I slammed the car door shut and walked into the lobby of the law firm.

"Can I help you?" asked the receptionist.

"Yes, I was hoping to speak to Miss Dawson. I realize I do not have an appointment but I just found out that my wife is cheating on me and I really need to consult with a divorce attorney."

"I am so sorry! What a horrible thing for you," the receptionist said sincerely with a warm sympathetic look on her face. "Well you are in luck. Miss Dawson's last appointment just canceled, so hold on and I will see if she will see you." After announcing my arrival to Annabelle the receptionist led me into her office.

"Hello, Mr. Cading. I am so sorry for your wife's infidelities. It's never easy when someone we trust betrays us. But I promise you that you've made the right choice coming to me," Annabelle said flashing a cheesy smile and way too much cleavage. I decided that she wasn't going to say anything to me if she knew I was working with Chloe or if she realized I was a cop, so my best bet to find out anything was to pretend that I just needed her help as a man going through a divorce.

"Well to be honest I'm looking around at different attorneys but I overheard the Governor arguing with his wife about what a great attorney you are."

Annabelle did not hide the shock on her face. "Kevin said that about me?" she said in a surprisingly soft and vulnerable voice. Her face immediately changed, "Well you should listen to him, he is the Governor after all and he knows what he's talking about. That wife of his is a complete bitch and no one should listen to a thing she says. She has so many people around here fooled but I have known her much longer than most people," she said with harsh distain in her voice. "She is worse than her twin sister," she mumbled to herself.

I felt my body immediately tense up, "Her sister," I said in a low rough voice. "I heard she was a wonderful person and she'd passed away due to a horrible attack. I also heard she was your friend," I said, not hiding my disdain for her that had appeared when she spoke poorly of my dead wife.

"I'm sorry!" she said her cheeks turning pink as she realized she had offended a future client. "She was at one point my friend. We had a falling out and it is just hard to think about her or really anyone in her family."

I tried to get the conversation back on the right track and hide my growing dislike of her. "So, you dislike the whole family?"

"They've never been great to me. But I don't dislike all of them. The Governor, well he has always been there for me in moments of need," she said with a faraway look in her eyes and sly smile on her face. She cleared her throat and seemed to come back to reality.

At that moment her entire body language changed on cue showing that she does this often as her face became full of seduction. "I'm so sorry Mr. Cading. I have completely gotten away from why you're here. You have nothing to worry though; we will drop that unpleasant subject and not bring it up again. Now we just need to focus on how I can help you," she said in a sultry voice as she moved from behind her desk and sat right on top of it placing her foot on the edge of my chair. "I think you'll find that not only will I get your divorce finalized I will also leave you very satisfied," she said while she slowly unbuttoned her top button and batted her eyelashes at me.

I quickly got up from my chair. "I don't know what type of man you think I am Miss Dawson, but you clearly have misjudged me. The only good thing that has come out of today's meeting is that now I know who not to vote for next election," I said as I exited the room ignoring Annabelle's surprised stricken face and her stutter of an apology. As I walked out to my car I couldn't help but think about what I had learned. Kevin and she are way closer then Chloe knows or for that matter anyone in town probably knows. What did she mean when she talked about him? It may be nothing, but for some reason it felt to me as if the answer to that question would answer a lot of other questions for both Chloe and myself. As I walked distracted to my car I forgot all about the vehicle that was following me before and did not even realize that from a distance it was still creeping behind me.

***

"This is Annabelle Dawson, how can I help you," I asked into the telephone still a little annoyed at myself for losing the last client.

"Annabelle why the hell are you speaking to Trevor Cading!" bellowed Kevin McDonald into the telephone.

"Well for your information he is one of my clients and anything that he says to me is privileged information. Why would you be interested in him anyways?"

"He is not going through a divorce, why would he be one of your clients?'

"Well little you know. It turns out his marriage is on the rocks and he needed to speak with me."

"You idiot, his marriage is not on the rocks!" Kevin screamed.

"Oh really," I screamed back. "How would you know anything about his marriage?"

"His marriage is not on the rocks because his wife is dead. He was Breanna's husband and he is working with Chloe to figure out what happened five years ago. Which means all of our dirty secrets will come out if we let them and do not play it smart."

"What?" I said completely stunned. "Breanna was married. When did she get married? How did I not know about this?" My mind was whirling. "Never mind, Kevin, I hate to remind you but you have more to lose than I do by our dirty secrets coming out."

"Really, Annabelle. I hate to remind you but I could ruin you in this town if any of that information gets out. We made a pact years ago and I will keep my part of the bargain and forget everything that happened and won't bring up anything, but if you screw me over then I swear on my mother's grave that I will ruin you!" he said in a quiet angry voice before he slammed the phone down.

Who knew what Kevin and I were starting eight years ago. We were just teenagers then; teenagers who did not think about consequences. Would I still make the same decisions if I knew that I would still be haunted by them now? I couldn't help but start smiling because I knew the answer. I definitely would have done the exact same thing.

***

Driving away from the law office, I tried to get my thoughts back to the case but it was hard to think of anything but that awful woman. Throughout the past years since Bre's death I have been through a lot but the one thing that I never had to deal with was anyone talking poorly of Breanna. Granted no one is a saint, not even Bre, but she was about as close to a saint as I have ever known and she definitely does not deserve a woman who claimed to at one point be her best friend talking badly about her. I shook my angry thoughts about Annabelle from my head and decided it was time to think about my next course of action.

My mind went back to figuring out the error in either the police or the hospital report. On the way to Annabelle's office I called and talked to the detective who wrote up the report. He told me he remembered the case like it was yesterday. When I asked him to pull up the two reports he got silent as he studied them carefully. He murmured with pain in his voice as if the memory hurt him that he could see it in his head and he clearly remembered that she was shot in her chest. He couldn't grasp how the medical examiner messed this up. He claimed that this is a mistake that could cost the doctor his job and I couldn't agree more. The more I've been thinking about everything the clearer its become that the only thing I can do is to go to visit the medical examiner at his office and see what he has to say about the critical error he made in his report.

I quickly called to see where I could locate Doctor Langing and learned that his office was located in the hospital and he would be there until 6:00, which gave me a good amount of time to head over there and question him. Breanna was brought to the Cape Cod Hospital to be examined by their medical examiner after she passed. It was not standard to transfer someone so far after they passed away, but the Judge and his wife said they were more comfortable with someone they knew examining their daughter's body.

I got to the hospital in no time and rushed over to his office. I saw him sitting at his computer with his hands zooming across the keyboard quickly typing up whatever he was working on. He was younger than I expected. He looked only to be in his early thirties, with sandy brown hair slicked down with hair gel and thick glasses. He jumped when he realized I was in the room with him. "Can I help you?" he asked in a jumpy voice. He came off as a very insecure man.

"I was just watching you type up what I assume is a report and was hoping that you wouldn't screw it up as much as you screwed up one of your past reports," I said to him matter of factly.

"I don't know what you mean," he said scrunching up his nose and pushing his glasses up looking truly puzzled as he stepped behind the desk. "Do I know you?"

"My name is Detective Cading and I'm talking about Breanna Cading's report, or as you may know her Breanna Patterson."

"Who?" He asked pretending to not remember examining a member of one of the most prominent families in the area.

"Are we really going to play this game? Are you actually going to sit here and play dumb? Why the fuck are you lying to me?"

His face immediately turned a shade whiter as I could tell he was searching for his words. "Look, fine I remember her but that was years ago. I have examined hundreds of people since her. So, I don't know what you are talking about. I just reported what I found, like I always do"

"Really, then explain to me as a doctor who graduated from Harvard Medical School how it is possible that you completely messed up the location of the bullet."

This time his face honestly looked confused as he took the report that he had written up from my hands. He sat down reading over what he wrote. He looked up at me with wide serious eyes, "Where was she shot?"

"Seriously! How would you not know the answer to that? Did you even examine her? What the hell happened here?" I screamed at him.

"Calm down detective," he said as sweat started to bead up on his forehead. "Look I had no choice, please don't report me", he said in a soft, desperate voice. "This job is my life."

"What do you mean you had no choice?"

"The judge, he dictated to me what to write. He was the one who told me where she was shot. He claimed he didn't want anyone to examine her body and he wanted her left alone. That is why he had her transferred to this hospital. I was new to the position and if I didn't do what he said then he was going to ruin me. No other doctor at any other hospital would of agreed to his request. Due to the nature of her death an autopsy was required but no other doctor would have pretended to examine her body if they didn't. Truthfully I wouldn't have agreed to his request but like I said I was new and he's very intimidating. I'm so sorry, I know what I did was not ethical but at the time I really was only trying to honor a man who had just lost his daughter."

"You were being a spineless coward, is what you were being. You do not have to worry though, the judge has ruined too many people's lives and I don't see the point in having him destroy another person. Your secret is safe with me as long as you promise nothing like this will ever happen again, because I can promise you that if it does I will ruin you."

I walked out of the room hearing the doctor's apologies in the distance. I could not seem to process what I had just learned. It was definitely not normal the parents not to want the medical examiner to study and report on their child. What does that mean? Why would the judge not want him to examine Breanna's body? Was this the real reason that he had her body transferred to Cape Cod Hospital? I know that I am clearly missing something but the million-dollar question is; what the hell is it?

***

"Annabelle is such a bitch." I couldn't help but think in my head. I really never gave her much thought but ever since I talked to Chloe about the past I couldn't seem to get her out of my mind. She always tries to ruin everything. I could never tell Chloe, but Breanna was not much better. The two of them together were the worst. They used to prance around the town acting as if they were so righteous. Breanna was constantly pulling the, I am Chloe's twin thing so I am so much better then everyone else. It was really getting old to everyone. It was obviously devastating when she died and I would do anything to help Chloe remember her past but I would never like Annabelle. All I could do now, though, is be the best friend possible to Chloe and if she needed help with anything I had to be here for her.

"Lily darling, is dinner ready?" I hurried into the kitchen to finish the final touches of the meal for my husband. I smiled, as I thought of Annabelle home alone by herself. No matter what she did in the past her life would never be as perfect as Chloe's and mine.

***

"What now?" I thought to myself as I massaged the creak in my neck. I had been writing down everything that I thought could help. I had read the police report, talked to Annabelle and tried to speak with Kevin and my parents. I had a feeling my secret hiding space held some of the answers. My phone jingled and, as I looked at the number, I felt a slight tremor of glee go through me when I saw Trevor's name appear on my caller ID.

"Hello," I said happily, as my front door slammed shut and I heard the heavy footsteps of Kevin walk into the house.

"Hey there," he said in a husky voice. "First of all I wanted to apologize in case you got in trouble with your husband earlier today."

"I honestly have no idea what you are talking about," I said trying to think of a reason that Trevor could have possible gotten me in trouble with Kevin.

"I called you earlier and he picked up. He didn't seem happy that I was calling you."

I rolled my eyes at Kevin's overly possessive behavior. "I'm sorry about that. You must have called when I went out for a run. I left my phone on the table. I'm sure he didn't mean to be rude."

He gave a little chuckle. "I am sure he did but that's ok. I was just calling earlier to tell you that I'm on the Cape. I was hoping we could meet for a drink later on tonight. I want to compare notes and see what we came up with."

"Hey babe, who are you on the phone with?" Kevin said as he finally made it into the living room. He made his way over to me and kissed my neck.

I waved him off feeling half annoyed that he didn't tell me that Trevor had called earlier and equally annoyed that he even answered my phone. He would have been furious with me if I had picked up his phone. "Yes that sounds wonderful," I said to Trevor. "When and where?"

"How about the Patio at 9:00?"

"Sounds great, see you there," I said hanging up the phone.

"Who will you see, where?" Kevin asked over my shoulder.

I made a quick decision that I was tired of lying and he is my husband so I should just go ahead and be honest with him. If he wants to be annoyed that's his prerogative but I pride myself on being honest so I'm going to stay that way. "I'm meeting up with Trevor later. If you want to come you are more than welcome, but we are going to compare notes on what we have found out so far involving the past. I think we are starting to make some progress and I'm excited that we are finally starting to find some real answers."

Kevin's whole body tensed up. "I thought we were on the same page with him. You know that I don't trust or like him."

"But why? You keep telling me you don't like or trust him but you've never given me a reason why you don't like him. He is my brother in law and I do trust him. He wants to find out what happened to Breanna, which goes hand in hand with what happened to me. I want to find out who did this to me."

"Chloe I understand that, but you have to trust me that Trevor is bringing nothing but trouble into our lives. I forbid you to go there tonight. This is for the best."

"Seriously? You forbid me? One thing I have learned over the past few weeks is that the real Chloe doesn't and didn't take orders from anyone. I gave you two options, one, you can watch me walk out that door or two, you can come with me. But don't sit there and act like you know what is best for me. What are you hiding Kevin? What is the real reason you don't want me to hang out with Trevor? Why don't you stop lying and tell me the truth.

Before I could react I felt Kevin's large hand slap me hard across my face. I fell down shocked and holding my stinging face, which I could tell was immediately turning red and swelling. "You want to know why I don't want you to meet Trevor. It's because he's questioning that whore Annabelle."

"What does she have to do with anything," I said with tears stinging my eyes, still clutching my swollen cheek.

"Don't be an idiot Chloe! Yes I fucked her. It happened years ago. But we both know that if that information gets out then my political career is over. Everyone looks at me as a family-man politician. The public needs to see that family values are important to me. You knew what you were getting into when you married me! You have always known that my political career is the most important thing in my life. I need you to stop questioning my every decision!"

He stopped for a second and looked at me with fire burning in his eyes, like he was studying me and trying to figure out how to fix the situation. "You have never been like this before. You've always listened to me. It wasn't until Trevor reentered the picture that you became disobedient. Although now that I think back, I've been telling you that I need to start a family for a while now. So it's time to make some changes. You are going to go back to listening and respecting me like you did before Trevor entered the picture and it's time you step up to the plate and get pregnant. I need children to keep up my image," he said with rage coursing through him and a look in his eyes that I had never witnessed and shook me to the core.

So this was his big secret; he cheated on me with Annabelle. I wasn't sure how to feel. I felt betrayed and hurt but it was hard to get my emotions under control and figure out what I was feeling while he was screaming at me. Lily was right, Annabelle is terrible but more than that so is my husband. I felt so confused about everything. The one and only thing I did know for sure was that for the first time in five years I felt scared of my own husband. "Kevin you're out of control I'm heading out and not coming back until you get under control," I said with a shaky voice as I started to get up and ignore the throbbing coming from my face. Trying to keep my calm I did not look at Kevin, just reached for my purse that was on the counter.

"No, you are not going anywhere. You must not have heard me before. I think it's time you start acting like a wife to me," Kevin said screaming, still completely out of control.

He reached for me and pulled me to him grabbing my waist with one arm and yanking at my clothing with the other. I realized what was happening and started screaming and trying to jerk away.

"Kevin get the hell off me!" I bellowed as I tried to jerk away from him. But I was helpless. All of a sudden I started to have a flash of something else, maybe a memory. Kevin was on top of me in the back seat of a car. I could hear Annabelle laughing in the distance. I was helpless to move as he tore off my clothes. I was crying and trying to shove him off of me as I felt him press himself to me and enter roughly inside of me. I squeezed my eyes shut, unable to scream, unable to process the horror that was unfolding. I kept going from past to present; Kevin and I in my living room; Kevin and I in a car. It seemed to be the same scenario, just one in the past and the other terror happening to my body right now. His secret about Annabelle was not that he slept with her, well maybe he did, but his other secret was that he raped me years ago before I lost my memory.

"Chloe look at me, Chloe are you with me?" I was brought back to the present. Kevin looking at me with fake concern on his face, my clothes ripped and scattered around the floor. I was shaking in shock and fear as Kevin pulled me onto the couch and into his arms and whispered, just sleep baby we will work this all out in the morning.

Chapter 12

I started to head to the Patio and, listening to my gut instincts, kept looking into the review mirror to see if I was being followed again. I was happy that Chloe agreed to meet with me. I really wanted to put our heads together and figure out what was going on with Annabelle. I really felt like she was holding something back from us. I mean, I'm sure she is. She really has no reason to tell the truth to either of us.

"Son of a bitch," I muttered to myself as I noticed the same car from earlier following me. Well it's time to put an end to this I thought to myself. I quickly turned around the corner and led my follower to the end of the alley. As I reached the end I jerked my car to a stop and jumped out and pulled my gun on the man behind me.

He quickly realized he was trapped and pulled his hands off of the steering wheel.

"Who the hell are you? Why are you following me?" I said, demanding an answer as I walked over to the driver side window.

"Aw man, I don't know what you are talking about," the short bulky man said. "I was just driving and got turned around. I mean no harm."

"Don't bullshit me! I'm a police detective, I am going to have your plates run and unless you start being straight with me I am going to arrest you right now."

"Ok, ok calm down. There is no reason to get all riled up. My name is Ethan Jenkins and I was asked by our Governor to watch you and make sure you weren't out to hurt his wife. I wasn't out to hurt you but to make sure that you weren't out to harm Chloe."

"I appreciate your concern, but Chloe is my sister-in-law and I can assure you she is safe, so you can leave now or get arrested."

After Ethan sped off I continued to the Patio. I was now going to be late. I quickly ran up to the front door of the Patio and searched around the bar for Chloe. Surprisingly I didn't see her. I grabbed a seat at the bar and waited. After three beers I was about to ask for my tab when I turned and saw Chloe walk into the bar. My heart stopped, not because she looked like my dead wife, not because, as much as I didn't want to, I thought she was beautiful, but because her face had a massive bruise on it and she looked as if she were in shock. I threw money down on the bar and rushed to her.

She avoided looking at my face. "Can we go somewhere more private," she said in a soft voice.

"Of course." I ushered her out to my car noticing that she was shaking. I could feel my body clenched up ready to attack whoever hurt her.

We got into my car and had a very silent car ride. I stopped when I realized that I had no idea where I should take her. My place was all the way out in Boston. "Why are we stopped? She whispered.

"Where do you want to go? Do you want me to take you home, or to your parents?"

"No," she said urgently, her face still pale from shock. "Let's go to Boston. We can talk at your place, then I will check myself into a hotel."

"Alright, although I do have a spare bedroom, you can feel free to just crash at my place." I paused, "unless of course you think it would upset your husband."

She flinched when I mentioned him. Which answered my question about who hurt her. I took a deep breath to restrain myself from saying something very nasty about him. When the time was right, though, he would be seeing me, and it would not be a pleasant visit. "I don't care what Kevin thinks. I need my space from him right now."

"Alright, well."

"Let's not talk right now. If you don't mind, I would just like to close my eyes for the rest of the car ride."

"Ok no problem, we can talk once we get there." My head was spinning the rest of the ride. Chloe's eyes were shut but I could tell she was not sleeping. Her right cheek had swelled up considerably more since we got into the car and I knew I had to get ice on it as soon as possible. As we pulled up to the apartment driveway Chloe immediately sat straight up and got out of the car moving like she was a robot. We walked into my place and she took a seat on the couch. I walked into the kitchen, grabbed a towel, filled it with ice and then sat in the leather chair across from her. I leaned forward and just waited for her to be ready to speak. She sat with her legs folded under her, one arm across her chest and the other pressing the ice against her face. She looked scared, guarded and confused all at once.

She finally took a deep breath and looked at me. "Thank you for bringing me here. I just needed to get away."

"Chloe what happened?"

"Kevin and I had a fight. I told him I was meeting you and he forbad me to come see you. He got crazy," she said looking away from me seeming to try to figure out everything in her head. "I asked him about Annabelle and he said he had an affair with her once but I just needed to drop that. It was in the past and we needed to move on. He got stuck on talking about his image and it turned from me questioning him to him accusing me that I wasn't doing my wifely duty in producing children for him. He claimed he wanted a child and we had to create a family that the public would like. Just another way for him to get more votes," she said with a little laugh. "We have never even talked about having kids until right then."

"What happened then," I asked tensely.

"He hit me and then raped me," she said with a dull look in her eyes. Then she looked at me square on, "that wasn't even the worse part."

"What was," I asked, scared to hear the answer. My heart was already pounding and I felt sick at what she was telling me. What could possibly be worse than finding out she had been attacked.

"The worse part is also the best part. It is ironic, I have wanted this for so long and now that it's starting to happen I just want it to stop."

"For what to stop, what happened Chloe?" I said with my voice slightly rising, feeling frustrated that I was having trouble following her train of thought.

"My memory, it has started to come back. But I wish it would just stay buried in the past because what I am remembering is not happy memories with my sister but awful things, terrible secrets. I remember what a horrible man I have married. Trevor, this is not the first time he has raped me. I remember, he raped me once before. He raped me once before, with Breanna's best friend Annabelle there laughing as it happened. Why the hell would I just choose to stay with a man that did that to me? And we know now how horrible of a person Annabelle is. How can a person witness something like that and just laugh?"

My heart was pounding with anger at Kevin and sympathy for Chloe. "Chloe this is not your fault. For all you know that could of happened right before the attack. I mean that would explain why you were coming to see Breanna. You were coming to get away from Kevin. Plus to make sure that Breanna would never talk to Annabelle again. But before we go into this anymore I need to get you to a hospital. You need to have a rape kit done and I need to make an official police report."

"No, I am not going to the hospital and I am not filing a police report. I need to stay focused. Plus, that will kill my parents and they have already gone through enough pain in their lifetime. Now that I have come this far and we have figured out this much, I need to keep going. I mean if Kevin is the type of man who would attack and rape his own wife who is to say he is not also the type of man that would burn down a house and kill my sister. I need to confront him again."

"Well not tonight you aren't. I don't agree with you not going to the hospital or filing a report but I'm not going to force you to do anything you don't want to do. I think for now the most important thing is for you to get some sleep," I said, leading her to the spare bedroom. After I got her settled I wished her sweet dreams and shut the bedroom door on a girl who looked still so lost and scared. Now that I was alone with my thoughts I couldn't help but think of all of the things I wanted to do to Kevin. I never liked him but it never even occurred to me that he could have killed my wife. He was a dirty politician, but a murderer? I guess everything is possible. One thing for sure is that Chloe will never go back to him. I will make sure of that. If she won't let me file charges against him I will make sure he pays in my own way.

***

I woke up, covered in sweat. I was crying, dreaming of both of the rapes, past and the present, over and over again. My phone was buzzing with missed calls and texts and is what must have woken me. I had a couple of missed calls from Lily and I had seventeen missed phone calls from Kevin plus a dozen or so texts from him saying how sorry he was and how he wanted me to come home so he could make it up to me. After he raped me I had pretended to fall asleep. When he thought I was out, he got up to use the bathroom and while he there I got up, sprinted to my car and zoomed out of there as fast as I could. Reading the texts just made me cry harder to the point where I was getting hysterical I had tried to keep it together but I could feel myself breaking. I didn't know what to do or how I should handle this. I didn't know how to keep myself together.

"Chloe," came Trevor's voice from the doorway as he knocked softly. "Are you ok? Can I come in?"

"I'm fine," I said, barely getting the words out in between sobs. With that, he walked in and scooped me into his arms pulling me onto his lap. I started to cry harder into his white t-shirt. I don't know how long I sat there crying but it felt good just to let go. I finally lifted my head from his shirt and looked into his eyes. Somehow in my vulnerability I couldn't help myself and I found myself kissing him. He froze for a second and then seemed to let go and returned my deep kisses. I clung to his t-shirt. It felt like my life depended on this, as if he pulled away then I would just completely fall apart again. His hands went under my t-shirt and his fingers caressed me. Our clothes seemed to just fall off on their own and I pulled him on top of me wishing for this never to end. I needed this to help me forget about all of the ugly stuff. He kissed my eyes, my lips, my chin down to my nipples. All at once he was in me, loving me, and everything seemed right in the world again.

In a flash he was in me again, but as before this was not the present but a memory of him making love to me. It was not violent, but passionate just like the current moment. Then it was not one flash, but many flashes of him making love to me and kissing me. I gasped when I realized what this meant and pulled myself away from him.

"You lied to me," I said in a shocked tone, jumping out of the bed and grabbing the sheet to cover myself. I felt just as violated by him as I did by Kevin. "I thought I could trust you, but you have been lying to me all of this time."

"Chloe I have no idea what you are talking about," he said in a soft but stern voice, clearly not wanting to upset me any further. His face was flushed from our passionate encounter and he looked sexier than I had ever seen him before, even in the past I am sure. "Calm down and let's talk about what you think I have lied to you about."

"You told me we had never met!" I said my voice shaking with rage. "I asked you straight out if we were lovers before going to that high school and you said no!"

"Chloe this is the first time we have ever made love. And while I understand how messed up this is, at the same time I don't regret it. For whatever reason it just feels right and I can't help the way I feel about you."

"Stay away from me you pig," I screamed stepping back from him. "My memories are coming back and I know that we have done this before. You are a liar and no better than Kevin!"

I grabbed my purse and went running to the front door.

"Chloe, where are you going? I drove you here!" He screamed after me as I ran out to the sidewalk.

"Trev Anthony stay the hell away from me or I swear to God I will be pressing charges against someone but it will be you not Kevin!" I ran as fast as I could down the street without looking back at him. I knew that there was a gas station only a few blocks from his place and I could easily call a cab from there. To my luck, as soon as I hit the main road a cab was driving past. I waved him down and hopped in.

"Where to lady?" the cab driver asked looking at me in his review mirror.

"That is a great question," I said to myself thinking, what the hell am I going to do now, as I sat dazed and in tears.

Chapter 13

I had been pacing all night. What the hell did I do? How could I let myself snap like that? It was like the past came back to the present. I never thought I could hurt the person I loved and the person I called my wife. Let's face it though; I have never been good at loving other people. If Chloe went to the police I would be ruined, it would be all over for me. I would of course deny the charges and claim that she had been depressed lately and that this must be an act of her depression. Even if they did believe me, my political career would be over and everything I had worked for would go down the drain.

I knew what I had to do. Ethan had called earlier and told me that Trevor had spotted him. I should have known not to trust a civilian to do the hard work. I took a deep breath and picked up my cell phone. I hated making this phone call but I knew it was the only way out of this mess for me.

After three rings he finally answered. "Kevin, do you know what time it is? Why are you calling me?"

"Sir, I am afraid we have an issue that needs to be dealt with immediately. I messed up and I messed up bad."

There was a long pause on the other end. "Messed up as badly as you did years ago? Years ago, when I had to clean up the awful mess you made?" he said in voice that could terrify even the strongest person.

I paused for a second. It was tough to know how much to tell him. Years ago, when I had screwed up so badly, I sugarcoated everything for the judge. He never knew how badly I had royally messed up. There was no reason for him to know the whole truth this time either. "No, not exactly. I am afraid that I snapped. It was Trevor's fault, really. He has been trying to pull Chloe away from us, her family. So I got angry and screamed. I screamed and I hit her. Basically, I scared her and now she is avoiding me," Telling him only what I had to. It wasn't actually a lie; I did scare her after all. I just wasn't telling him all of the ugly details.

"How the hell could you let this happen Kevin? You know I don't like this. I want Chloe safe and happy. I definitely do not want her scared of her own husband. And I should knock you out for laying a hand on her. She has been through enough in her lifetime and for you to harm her." He left it there. "She is the only daughter I have left!"

"I understand that, sir, and I can promise you that this will never happen again."

"It better not, or staying Governor of Massachusetts will be the least of your problems. We don't want me to choose someone else for the position, do we Kevin?"

"Of course not judge, and thank you for fixing my mistakes yet again, you are the best father in law that a guy can ask for."

***

"Hello," Chloe said in a soft, broken voice. It almost tore me apart to hear her this way. I have made many mistakes in my life but trusting Kevin to be a good person and a good fit for my daughter may have been one of the biggest ones. I did make that decision years ago, though, and he is the Governor now and great for the family, financially and publically anyways.

"Chloe it's me, where are you?"

"Oh daddy!" she said and then started to cry quietly. "I am in the back of a cab heading back to P-town from Boston. Kevin and I got into a fight and I'm not going back there right now."

"I understand sweetie, why don't you come here? You mother is asleep, so you can come and sleep in your old bedroom and in the morning we can all sit down and help you figure out this mess with Kevin. I can even give Lily a call if you would like and you two can have a sleepover like when you were kids. Would you like that?

"Thank you daddy, I should be there in 20 minutes. Don't call Lily. I don't want to make her leave Don in the middle of the night and please, please don't ask Kevin to come over! I don't want to see him and I think it will be good for me to try to sort out the evening's events by myself."

"Of course, just tell the cab driver to drive safely and I will see you soon."

"Thank you daddy, I love you so much."

"I love you too Chloe, see you soon." I hung up the phone feeling like a traitor. How can I, as her father, continue to stand up for Kevin? I figured the first time he messed up it was a one time only disaster. I knew he could be dangerous but I never imagined after the accident that he would ever harm her. I definitely did not peg him as someone who would hit his wife. Thank God she never knew about everything he did to her in the past.

I just felt sick to my stomach thinking about all of the stuff I've done in my life. Everything from covering up Kevin's crimes against my daughter and, then of course, my own crime I had to commit later on.

***

My cab pulled up to my parent's house. I threw the cabbie some money and started walking slowly up to the front door. What was I going to say to my parents? I just felt so lost and confused. It was a comfort walking to a safe place but I really didn't want to devastate my parents by telling them what a creep their son in law, who they adored, was. I almost had to laugh at myself. What a creep he was– look at what a creep I was! I had an affair with my sister's husband before the accident and cheated on my boyfriend. I just needed to lie down and decide where I should go from here. Maybe I should go back to Kevin, he may be an awful person but I don't seem to be much better. No matter what I decide the only thing I know for sure is I am not in a place to make any decisions tonight.

I let myself in with my key and was immediately hugged by my mom and dad. They were both looking at my face in horror. I felt bad that they had to see me like this. I quickly explained what happened to my face by coming up with a lame lie on the spot. I said I had tripped on a high heel and hit my face on the banister. Part of me just wanted to start crying again but I think I was just too exhausted to do anything anymore. "Chloe sit down. I will get you a glass of wine and some Advil for your face," said my mom, who my father had woken up to tell I was coming over.

"Thank you, but no thanks," I said with a small smile. "I really just want to lay down and sleep for awhile. Can we talk in the morning? I'm not up for it tonight."

"Of course," said dad. "It's very late and you'll feel much better with a good night's sleep behind you."

I walked into my old bedroom with my father behind me. I quickly climbed under my down comforter and felt my eyes closing as I watched my father shut the curtains of my room to make sure that the morning light did not wake me from the deep sleep that was sure to overtake me any second.

***

I was running from Kevin's car with tears streaming down my face. I was shaken to the core. I quickly came to a stop because I could not seem to breathe. I looked back at where I was attacked and there was Annabelle hopping into Kevin's car, laughing and throwing on her sunglasses as Kevin sped off in that stupid black convertible of his. I didn't know where to go or what to do. I needed to feel safe and alone with my thoughts for just a little bit. There was only one place I could think of that would give me that comfort. I ran as fast as I could back home to my parent's house and once I got there I snuck as quietly as possible in through the back door. I could hear the television on in the living room and was sure my father was watching the baseball game. I knew my mother was in the kitchen because I could hear the clatter of the pots and pans. I quietly made my way into my father's study and snuck into my sister's and my secret hiding place. Once I was in the safety of our room I slid against the cold hard wall to the floor and just cried for what seemed like forever.

I must have dozed off at one point because I woke to my father yelling to my mother that he would take the phone call in the office. My dad still did not know about our private room because both my sister and I had made sure to be careful. We had overheard many private conversations over the years from our little spot. During our eavesdropping we had heard everything from my dad's business calls to my parents talking about what presents to give us for Christmas. It was how we found out there was no Santa and how we found out what an important job our daddy had as a judge.

"Kevin, what can I do for you son?" I froze, why would Kevin be calling my dad? He surely could not be confessing to my father what he did to me. My father would kill him. He would go to jail for a long time. Maybe it was better this way, I would not have to tell everyone what had happened. He would tell my dad and my dad would send him away and I would never have to see his disgusting face again.

"Wait a minute, slow down Kevin, what the hell happened?" He was doing it, he was telling my dad. My heart was pounding so hard in my chest I felt like I was going to faint or my heart would explode. I took a deep breath and then when I thought about it I almost breathed a sigh of relief waiting for my dad to give it to him. He would take care of everything like he always has. My dad is the one person that I have always been able to count on for anything and everything. Now in my time of need he would make sure this monster paid for the crime he committed against me.

"Kevin you son of a bitch! How could you do this? How could you hurt my daughter! You have ruined everything!" He paused listening to Kevin's response. Ruined everything? That was a weird way to respond.

"Listen, we will work this out. I haven't seen her yet, so maybe she hasn't told anyone. As long has no one else knows then everything should be ok. I still think you will make the perfect addition to this family and I know that everyone makes mistakes. Just do not let this happen again. Do you understand me? I am letting you into this family and as a family we protect each other. No more screwing up."

They continued to talk for the next few minutes but I could hardly listen. I felt violated all over again. I had to hold my mouth to keep from getting sick and blowing my secret hiding spot. How could my father do this to me? How could he not stand up for me and send Kevin to jail. He works in the legal system; his job is to make sure the guilty are punished. Everything that I had ever thought about him was destroyed. He was not the man I thought he was, he was not the perfect father, the perfect person, the person I grew up looking up to as my role model. How is life so screwed up, people are never who I thought they were. I just curled up in a ball and lay there crying. I heard my father walk out of the study and I felt my crying get more hysterical.

I sat up quickly. The room was dark, where was I? I took a deep breath and took in my surroundings. I was sitting in my bed in my parent's house. I was not a young, lost woman anymore sitting in our secret room. Was it possible? Was that a memory? I hoped to God it wasn't because I knew what that meant. That meant that my father has known all these years why I drove to Breanna's house. I drove there because my father was a liar and a fraud. As much as I wanted to believe that was just a dream, I knew in my heart that it was not. That was a memory; clear as day now, the memory of me on the secret floor crying.

With that I felt the tears start to flow again. Was there no one in my life I could trust? I had my mom but all of this would kill her. The men have done so much to protect her from all of this and I now understand why, the truth was just too painful, to awful. I needed to think and clear my head. Where should I go, what should I do? I knew that the relationship I had with my father was officially over. I want nothing more from him. I couldn't run out though, my mother would know something was wrong.

I will just get up, go to breakfast and tell my mom that I'm fine. Kevin and I got into a fight but after a good night sleep I feel much better. I will send Kevin to Washington DC and make him travel around Massachusetts until after the election. After he gets reelected, which he most definitely will, I will officially separate from him and move into my own place. I will wait until then out of courtesy to him. I did, after all, cheat on him. If I was right and I was rushing to Trev's and Breanna's house after Kevin attacked me that meant I cheated on him before all of that. Who knows? Maybe he found out about my affair and that is why he got nasty with me that day. That could be why he initially attacked me. It would definitely explain why he hates Trevor so much.

"Honey, you ok in there?" my mom said as she knocked on the door.

"Yea mom, I am fine," I replied wiping the tears from my face. "Let me just get cleaned up and I'll be right down." I quickly cleaned up although I did give myself a few extra minutes to let the hot water soak into my skin to calm me down some. I was dreading having breakfast with my father. Sadly, I would rather just go to Boston and relax with Trevor. But he had lied to me too and I knew I had to live my life and I could not run away from it. So I took a deep breath, put my pearls back on along with my fake smile and plenty of concealer to hide the bruise on my face and walked down the stairs.

As I walked in the kitchen I was surrounded with smells of bacon, eggs and coffee. I breathed a sigh of relief when I saw my mom sitting at the table reading the paper alone.

She looked up and her eyes crinkled in a smile. Oh honey, you look so much better this morning. I knew all you needed was a good night's sleep." She jumped up and gave me a quick hug. "Now grab a cup of coffee and have some breakfast. Your father had to run a couple of errands this morning but promised to be home soon."

I sat down and decided to take a risk. "Mom, I have something to tell you and I don't want you to freak out or anything but it is very new."

"Ok," she said slowly lowering her coffee and leaning into me, her face turning very serious. "You can tell me anything."

"Alright," I said slowly, deciding where to begin. I decided that there was nowhere to begin but to just blurt it out. "I'm starting to get my memory back."

My mom looked like she was in shock and took a deep breath. While I couldn't tell what she was thinking the shock in her eyes was unmistakable. "What?" she asked startled. She got up and started to clean her breakfast dishes. She was acting nervous and fidgety.

"I thought you would be happy mom," I said confused by her reaction.

"I am Chloe, of course I a```m happy," She replied turning around. She seemed to be reading my face. "What do you remember?"

"Just bits and pieces really. It just keeps coming back to me in dreams and in flashes."

"Oh," my mom said smiling and looking relaxed again. "Then you don't remember the fight."

"The fight?" I asked confused. "What fight?"

"I am sorry, I should have told you about this a long time ago. I just always felt so horrible about it. I mean it was really silly. It's just, the last time I saw you before the accident we got into a huge argument. I said some really terrible things to you. You told me that you were considering taking a year off from college and traveling Europe for a year after the wedding. I thought it was a bad idea, I just wanted you to finish your degree and graduate, then you could travel around Europe. Plus you hadn't talked about it with Kevin and I thought it was a bad idea to keep something so huge from him. And well, I also had a horrible day that day, and I was just very mean to you. I'm so sorry. It just killed me that when I thought I was going to lose you that the last memory we had together would be of us fighting."

I thought back to when I woke up in the hospital, I remember her tortured face. It made sense now. She was thinking about our last fight. "Oh, mom don't worry, that is long in the past and I don't even remember it. It couldn't have been too important or too upsetting or I think I would have remembered it by now. But even when I do remember it, I promise you I will still forgive you for anything you may have said, and I of course apologize for anything I said to you back then."

My mom laughed and took my hand. "That does seem silly doesn't it? Well onto more important topics. Are you ready to talk about what happened last night? You were so distraught. Your father said something happened between you and Kevin, nothing serious I hope?"

"No mom, nothing serious," I said patting her hand. "Nothing that we can't work through."

"Oh good," she said opening her paper back up. "That would be a travesty for our family. He's so wonderful and such a good son in law and it would be such a public scandal if something major happened between you two. So even if it takes a week or so for you two to patch things up please keep a smile on in front of the cameras."

"Of course mom," I sighed, such a typical response from the people in my life. It doesn't matter what goes wrong, or how I feel, just keep smiling for the public. All of sudden I felt so tired again. "Mom I know I just got up but I don't think I slept as long as I should have. I think I am just going to lie down for a nap and take it easy for a while if that's ok with you.

"Of course honey, last night was stressful for you and stress can be exhausting It's a good idea for you to get a lot of sleep, it will keep you from getting dark circles under your eyes."

"Yes mom, that is exactly what I was worried about," I mumbled while rolling my eyes and walking back up to my bedroom. I could hardly even drag my body back into my bed. It was like all of sudden everything that I was stressing about and everything that had happened was dragging me down and my mind and body were so exhausted. I rolled into my bed too tired to even take my shoes off. I fell into a very deep sleep.

***

As I was driving to the bank I could not shake how guilty I felt. Chloe looked absolutely awful last night. She looked completely broken. It was heartbreaking to see. I know everyone makes mistakes but the sins that Kevin and I have committed can never be forgiven. I knew that what is done is done and the only thing I could do now is try everything in my power to support Chloe and work on helping her regain her happiness. I had to believe that she would land back on her feet like she always does. Maybe I could buy a cruise for her and Kevin to take after the election, give them a break and a chance to rebuild their relationship.

Hopefully she would be awake when I returned so I could suggest it. I had to fix this mess. I've caused her too much pain in her life, and as her father I had to try to bring her some happiness. This at least I could possibly fix. What I did in the past I could unfortunately never make right. So I would make everything else right. I took a deep breath, zoomed down the street and tried to clear my head a little.

***

When I finally woke up I felt like I had slept for a year. I took a deep sigh of relief while I stretched out in my bed.

For the first time in awhile I had no dreams or memories hurtling down on me while I slept. I guess my brain knew I needed a break for one day. I stood up and stretched my body. I looked out the window and could hardly believe what I saw: it was dark outside. I had slept literally all day. I grabbed my phone off the nightstand and turned it back on. I was not surprised to see I had a million missed calls from both Trevor and Kevin. I was surprised to see it was 8:00pm. I knew it was about time for me to face the real world but I still was not quite ready for that.

I tip toed downstairs quietly. Just like this morning, my mom was sitting at the kitchen table. This time, though, instead of drinking a cup of coffee she had a cup of tea in front of her. "Thank God," she exclaimed when she saw me. "I was just thinking of calling the doctor. I knew a nap was good for you, but I didn't expect you to sleep all day!"

"I know mom, me either. But I'm feeling much better now. I just needed to rest and not think of anything else. I think now I am just going to go for a walk before I head back to my life and the real world."

"Ok, but don't be gone too long because your father just ran out and will be right back. He's just as worried about you as I am and he wants to make sure you're ok. You are ok right? You didn't remember anything else too unpleasant or anything else you want to share with me?"

"No mom, but I do have a strong feeling that, whether I want to or not, I will be remembering everything that happened the night of the fire really soon. Once I do remember, though, maybe we can finally put everything behind us and I can get on with my life. Anyway I will come back in after my walk but I then think I am going to head out and go back to my house."

"Ok, well we'll see you after your walk then. And who knows, maybe you have remembered everything you will remember. Maybe there is just nothing else to remember."

"Thanks mom, but I kind of doubt that," I said as I walked to the front door.

I started to head towards the beach. Nothing calms me more and seems to erase all of my worries than a long walk on the beach. As a last thought I reached into my car, opened my center console and grabbed my mace and stuck it in my pocket. P-town is one of the safest places that I could imagine but you can never be too safe. I mean, let's face it, if I am not safe in my own home then I'm definitely not safe on a beach alone. I decided that once I figured everything out I was definitely going to take a self-defense class. I started walking down to the beach and began clearing my head. I felt the migraine that had started last night begin to fade away with each crash of the waves. I wasn't sure who I could trust anymore. I didn't even know if I trusted myself. I knew I need to allow myself to remember everything else from my past but a huge part of me just wished that the memories would stop coming back and I could go back to my sheltered life. I was once told that ignorance is bliss and I never believed that statement more than at this moment. For now I just wanted to keep meditating and focusing only on the ocean and nothing else.

After I had walked pretty far, I stopped and turned and just stared at the ocean for a while. The moon was almost full and the sky was clear with a million stars dancing above me. Now that my eyes had adjusted to the night the beach didn't seem so dark under all of the bright lights. It helped me to think that Breanna was with those stars watching me. I felt ashamed at the affair I had with Trevor but at the same moment I had to believe she was looking down on me forgiving me for all of my transgressions.

Then in a moment of insanity I emptied out my pockets, took off my shoes and walked straight into the ocean. The freezing water stung my skin and I knew that this was nuts. I just wanted to not think for once, I just wanted to swim in the cold ocean and push myself through the waves. I kept swimming for what seemed like a long time and all of a sudden I ran right into something. I lifted my head, took a deep breath of air and tried to focus on what was in front of me. Before I could take in the figure in front of me I felt a hand go crushing down on my head pushing me under water. I tried to fight the person who was above me. I managed to kick him. I felt my attacker back up for a second and I was able to gulp in a breath of air and felt some salt water go into my mouth. I tried to cough the water out of my lungs and I felt the person's hands on my head again pushing me under. I did my best to fight the darkness that was falling over me but I felt myself getting weaker as my lungs were burning with desire for oxygen. In my semi-consciousness I felt the person's hands come off of me. I was still too weak to raise myself up from the crashing waves. Right before I felt the final wave of darkness crash over me I felt the person pulling me up and onto the shore. I wasn't sure what they wanted from me, but I was unable to ask because the blackness engulfed me.

The next thing I knew I was coughing up water and taking deep breaths of air as I stared into Trevor's face. He was pushing into my chest with a look of panic on his face. "Hey, hey," he said pulling me up into a sitting position on the sand as I continued to cough up water.

I sat there confused for a second just staring at him as he tucked my wet hair behind my ears looking at my face so concerned. What had happened? How did I end up sitting here on the sand with Trevor? As I remembered everything I sat up more rigidly and as fast as I could I used all my strength and jumped up. It didn't matter that I didn't have my shoes on, or that I had left my phone and mace on the sand where I had started my swim. Trevor had just tried to kill me. That is all I could think about as I started sprinting towards my house fueled up with a rush of adrenaline.

Chapter 14

I sat there confused as I watched her run to the house. Why the hell was she running away from me? Thank God I came to explain everything to her when I did. I traced her phone, which I am legally not allowed to do but I had felt like it was worth the risk. When I saw her phone in the sand I assumed she had gone for a walk and left her stuff in a pile. I strolled down to the ocean thinking I would just wait when I saw the splashing in the water. I thought at first that it was a bird diving or maybe a seal hunting. I turned on my flashlight to be sure then realized in horror what was happening. I ran as fast as I could into the ocean praying that I got to her fast enough. When I got her out of the water she just laid limp in the sand. I don't think I had ever been that scared in my life. I performed CPR on her for a good thirty seconds, which felt like a million years, before she responded.

I now watched as she ran frantically as fast as she could when it hit me. She doesn't know that I just saved her life; she thinks that I tried to kill her. As I sat there digesting that I realized I could not let her continue to believe all of these things she was thinking. Besides, I needed to find out who was trying to hurt her. I saw the person in the wetsuit swimming away as I rushed in to save her. I had two options: go after her attacker or save her. I chose to save her. She was in danger and of course I was going to try to protect her. I have failed her so many times already and I would not let myself fail her again. I got up quickly and started to run after her. She had gotten a decent head start and I finally reached her as she was climbing the front steps of her parent's house.

"Please stop," I yelled as I sprinted up the front steps towards her.

"No you stop," she screamed back at me as she opened the front door. "Why did you come here? I asked you to leave me alone!"

"Chloe, Chloe what's wrong?" We both turned our heads to Kevin's voice. Kevin and her father came running into the living room.

Looking at Kevin I felt a huge surge of rage go through me. I lunged at him punching him square in the jaw. He crashed backwards into the coffee table smashing it into little pieces. He quickly got back up and lunged back at me, "You son of a bitch." He dove into my stomach throwing me into the wall. He punched my face and I gave him a blow to the stomach.

"Stop it, dad make them stop! Kevin and Trevor, please, enough!" I heard the voice of the woman I loved screaming.

"Boys stop it right now, I'm not kidding," screamed the judge. That made us both stop and take a deep breath.

"I'm sorry sir, but you have no idea what this man has done," I said still glaring at Kevin. I did not even dare look at her as she stood there just crying.

The judge went to her and hugged her towards him. "I have no idea what is going on but I know Chloe is wet and freezing cold and probably could use a nice hot shower. The stress of everything that is going on already put her in a coma-like sleep today and I don't think she can handle anymore."

I glanced at her. She seemed to be an emotional wreck and she also seemed to be pushing herself away from the judge while hugging her soaking wet body. I felt myself shaking with anger as I managed to get out the next sentence, "Your honor, this man who claims to be your son in law is an evil liar. He raped my wife and just tried to kill her."

I turned towards the judge expecting to see a ton of anger as well as shock and confusion. Instead I saw something completely different. The anger, shock and confusion were there on some level but what I was not expecting to see was fear on his face as well.

I took in a deep breath. It felt like someone had punched me when I realized the truth. "You already knew."

***

I stood there pushing my father's arms away from me as Trevor and Kevin fought each other. I really didn't want my father's comfort, all I wanted to do was climb back into my secret room and just hide for the rest of my life. I heard Trevor proclaim that Kevin had raped his wife and tried to kill me. I felt my father's arms grab me and tighten around me. My crying came to a stop, I knew that my father knew about my rape many years ago. Did Kevin rape Breanna too? Also, what did he mean that Kevin just tried to kill me? Was I wrong in assuming that Trevor had attacked me? Was this just some way for Trevor to get the heat off of himself? Kevin was here at the house, there was no way he could have attacked me and then gotten back here fast enough.

I looked towards Trevor filled with confusion. His eyes looked fierce. He looked at me and looked like he was ready to jump in front of a bullet for me. I knew right then that there was no way he could have attempted to hurt me. In fact, he must have just saved my life. I would be dead right now if it weren't for him.

He then looked at my father and Kevin with such extreme hate in his eyes. He reached for my hand and I felt him pulling me towards him. "I don't understand," I whispered. I looked at Kevin, I looked at my father and I felt Trevor pulling me behind him, away from my father and Kevin. My father tried to hold on to me but Trevor won the battle quickly. I felt like I was in a movie and I should do something but I felt frozen like a statue. It also felt so comfortable to be in Trevor's arms but I felt so baffled by what was going on.

"You have known all this time but have just hid the truth from her," Trevor said his voice still shaking with anger. He must have just figured out that my father new about Kevin raping me. Well I guess it was bound to come out at some point. I was just not expecting it to be so soon.

"Listen Trevor, what happened between Breanna and me is ancient history, the judge was just trying to protect Chloe and my future. Chloe baby," Kevin said stepping towards me. "Please come on, I have made tons of mistakes but I will get help I promise."

"You raped Breanna?" I asked in a hushed voice staring at the man who I had slept next to every night for the past five years.

"Wait a minute!" screamed the judge. "I will not let this go on for one more second. What do you mean that Kevin raped Breanna? Don't go spreading vicious lies. Yes, Breanna and Kevin messed up. Kevin cheated on Chloe with Breanna. It was stupid of both of them but it was not rape, it was consensual."

"Sweetheart don't let Trevor fool you." Kevin chimed in. "I made a mistake but you forgave me for it years ago. He is just trying to stir things up again. Apparently one sister wasn't enough for him, he now wants the other."

"Baby he raped you," Trevor said. "And he will never lay a hand on you again or even get close to you."

"Trevor," I said pulling away from him. "I know that Kevin hurt me, and I'm trying to deal with things, although I didn't know that he slept with Breanna," I said turning towards him and wondering how are family could possibly be even more messed up.

"Chloe baby, I'm so sorry," Kevin said interjecting.

My dad just stood there, now glaring at Trevor with hate and fear in his eyes. "Trevor I think it's time you get out of our house. Our family has some stuff that we need to work out and you are not welcome here."

"Everyone stop!" Trevor screamed. "Baby," Trevor said pulling me in front of him. "There is no easy way to say this so I'm just going to trying to piece it together for you. "Why did you call me Trev Anthony when you were angry with me?"

"I don't know," I said remembering that I did indeed yell that at him.

"Babe, there is only one person who has ever called me that. And it was always when she was angry with me. That person was Breanna. That person is you."

I just stood there confused, trying to figure out what he was telling me.

"Honey" he said with sympathy filling his face. "You are Breanna," Trevor said in a hushed voice as if he was trying to protect me from his own words.

CHAPTER 15

I just stood there frozen for a minute. I couldn't comprehend anything anyone else was saying to me. I just saw all my memories come flashing back to me. Me as a little girl, "Breanna you are my best friend," Chloe saying to me. The memories flooded all the way to me making love to Trevor. I never slept with my sister's husband; I slept with my own husband. Everything made sense now. I felt myself slowly walking to the couch and sitting down and I continued to remember everything. I turned my head towards Trevor, Kevin and my dad. Trevor just had a look of love and concern on his face, Kevin looked like he had just had a huge bomb dropped on him and my father, his face was the face that confused me the most. He just had a look of guilt on his face.

"Daddy?" I said confused, looking for answers. It was bad when I thought he had kept the rape from me. I felt a surge of relief now that I knew that he didn't know Kevin raped me but instead believed I had an affair with Kevin. I jumped to conclusions too fast five years ago just like I did yesterday. I refuse to do that again. I need to stop assuming the worst in my family. There is no way he would have known this, no way he would have kept this from me and from everyone else.

"Chloe, this is ridiculous. You know that you are Chloe. Don't let this man confuse you. He just misses Breanna and is trying to confuse you. You are Chloe and you are married to Kevin." He turned his attention to Trevor. "You need to leave this house right now. I never want to see you again, and more importantly, you need to stay as far away from Chloe as possible. I will place a restraining order on you."

I looked at my father and I couldn't lie to myself. It was all over his face and how he was acting. While he did not know Kevin raped me he definitely knew that I was not Chloe. He had known my real identity all along.

"Honey," Kevin said looking at me. "What are you thinking?" As Kevin stepped towards me Trevor jumped in front of me in a protective stance. He looked like a lion ready to pounce on his prey. I don't know if I have ever seen someone have such a strong look of hate in their eyes. I also could see how much Trevor loved me, and with every painful memory that rushed through my mind, I had a flood of wonderful memories of Trevor and myself that came rushing back.

We met at an animal shelter. We were both volunteering there every Saturday and one day we were both heading out around noon and my car wouldn't start. He waited with me until AAA arrived to tow my car and then he drove me home. We ended up stopping and having lunch and we fell in love almost immediately. Our wedding was small, just us and a couple of friends at city hall but it was the most special day of my life. As my head spun with a flood of memories coming back I couldn't help but smile at that one. I lifted my head and stared at the man I loved more than anything in the world. It makes sense now why my memories started coming back the day I ran into him again. He was my whole world. He never stopped loving me even when he thought I was dead.

I turned my gaze from Trevor and I stared at Kevin. I almost felt sorry for him, the past five years had been a lie to him as well. We were both deceived by my father. Although when I thought of how he hurt me my feelings of sympathy for him immediately disappeared. I looked at my father and felt anger and hurt mixed all together into one.

"I'm not confused anymore, Trevor's right. I remember everything." I said almost in whisper. "I know it now. I am not Chloe, I am Breanna. Daddy," I whispered with tears in my eyes, "you knew this, how could you know the truth and not tell me?"

"Is this real?" Kevin asked me, shocked. He looked at my dad in disbelief.

"She doesn't have anything to say to you," Trevor said. "You are despicable. A disgrace as a human being, stay far away from her. It was you out in the ocean wasn't it?"

"I have no idea what you are talking about, I have been here for the past hour. Clearly I didn't do anything. I have made many mistakes, that is true, but I cannot believe that she is not Chloe. She is my wife! We have been married for the past four years. We made vows to each other to love each other in better or worse. Yes, this is the worse but we will make it through this. I don't care if you think that you used to be Breanna, you are Chloe now and that is the way it is going to stay."

"She also made those vows to me. She made those vows to me knowing who she was and meaning them. In the state of Massachusetts it is illegal to be married to more than one person. You out of everyone should know that *Governor.* Therefore you have never been married. Bre, come with me now, we'll head back and figure everything out. We'll figure out everything together."

I sat still on the couch, staring at Trevor. I was not sure about many things right now but the one thing I was sure of was him. I took the hand that he held out to me. "Kevin, Trevor is right. I'm Breanna. I didn't know it until right now but I remember," I said as tears filled my eyes. "I don't remember everything, but one thing I know for sure is that I'm not Chloe. And Dad," I said as I choked up. "You knew. You knew this whole time. I know why I left here and while I left under false assumptions, we could have worked that out. How could you have denied me my identity? Father's are supposed to love their children equally and you have come out and basically said that you love Chloe more by pretending I was her this whole time," I said, no longer controlling the tears and letting them stream down my face. Trevor pulled me close trying to help me stay in one piece.

"Chloe, you have to understand," my father said stepping to me.

I held my hand up to him to stop him from speaking. "My name is Breanna! You should know, you are the one who named me! I can't listen to this or you anymore. Please, I have heard enough for today and I need to leave and process all of this." Kevin looked at me with a mixture of confusion and pain in his eyes.

Trevor looked down at me. "Come on baby, let's go home." As Trevor led me out to my car, away from everything that had been my life for the past five years, I had never felt so emotionally drained in my entire life.

***

I watched the woman who I believed to be my wife walk past me out the door with another man, and for the first time in my life I felt my heart break a little. The judge and I hardly looked at each other as I grabbed my keys and walked out the door. I was hoping that he still believed me that Breanna and I had gotten drunk together and made a bad decision. It had worked out so perfectly when Breanna had fled town. The judge just assumed she was ashamed of our affair. But regardless of what the judge believed, I couldn't understand why he had lied to me all of this time about Breanna being Chloe. I guess it would make sense that he would prefer me to Trevor as a son in law. It would also make sense that he would want his only living daughter to be living close to him.

I went home without her and paced around my room all night long. I could not sleep in this house without her. I have treated Breanna horribly. There is no reason she should ever forgive me or even to stop hating me. She actually left the place she grew up in because of me. She probably thinks I deserve to be in jail and she's probably right. I know I need to change and I probably need help to do it. I have a position, though, where I'm in the public eye and I cannot allow this scandal to hit the press.

The first thing I need to do is win back my wife. I can convince her that, while we have had our bad times and I have messed up horribly more than once, she has stayed with me for the past five years for a reason and I believe the reason is that she loves me. She has been with me married, legally or not, for longer than she was ever with Trevor. No one has to ever know that she is not the real Chloe. Breanna died when she lost her memory five years ago and I can hopefully convince her that is for the best. There is only one way, though, that she will ever listen to me and agree to meet with me right now. I picked up the phone and dialed the number of someone who has everything to gain by keeping the secret and convincing my wife that she should remain as Chloe.

The phone rang a few times and a voice that answered while recognizable didn't sound familiar. Normally, the voice on the other end of the phone would sound strong and have a tone that would intimidate even me on occasions. Today I heard the weak voice of someone who was broken and falling apart. "Judge I think I know how we can fix our problem and get Chloe back."

***

The phone rang a few times and I answered feeling unrealistically hopeful that the person on the other side was my daughter telling me that she forgives me. I realize that what I did was extremely selfish but I only did it to keep my remaining daughter in my life. How could that be considered wrong?

"Hello," I said, my voice sounding more tired and worn out than I would have liked. Unfortunately it was not my daughter but the man I have called my son in law for the past five years, the man who was accused of horrible crimes tonight. I had to choose to believe that they were the ranting's of a desperate man who missed his wife. I could not trust that anything he said was true because the truth was too dreadful to believe. I listened to his plan for how we could get Chloe back, and while it seemed impossible, it was at least a plan and a possibility that our lives could stay exactly the way we wanted them to be. "Kevin I'm in, I will help you in whatever way I can to make this happen."

"What does Kevin want?" said the voice of my angry wife behind me. I had to unfortunately tell her everything after everyone stormed out. She cried for a while and her tears turned into anger. She screamed at me for a long time, telling me how selfish I was. Now, though, she has turned to acceptance and told me she understands why I would want our remaining daughter to be near us.

"Kevin has come up with a plan to keep Chloe in our lives. It is actually perfect. We know she will meet with us, and once we can get her here, one-on-one, away from Trevor, we can convince her that if this scandal gets out it will hurt the entire family. Our family shame will be on every magazine cover and website and everyone she has loved her whole life will be hurt. Kevin never knew about the switch and he fell in love with her. None of this is his fault. I only lied to keep her nearby. How can she blame me for that? Its perfect! We'll have our daughter back, Trevor will be out of our lives and the public will not know a thing."

For the first time all day I felt like a huge weight had been lifted off my chest. I finally could see that things could possibly work out. I was not going to be the scandal that P-town talked about for decades and my family was not going to fall apart. I felt sinfully happy and I looked at my beautiful wife beaming.

"Honey I see that this is making you feel a lot better. But I think we need to be realistic. Chloe," she paused for a second and as she rubbed her forehead. "Or I mean Breanna, crap this is hard. Well whatever we are supposed to call her, our daughter she is furious with you. While she probably would agree to meet with me there is no way she will meet with you and Kevin away from Trevor. I think that even if I told her it would just be me she was meeting with she would still have her guard up and would insist that Trevor came along."

"Oh honey, I would not have you call Chloe and lie to her telling her that she was meeting with you. I would like to keep you as out of this as much as possible. I feel terrible that you have had to endure all the pain that I have caused and I would like to fix this mess without involving you."

"Well than how do you plan to get her to come see you both?" she said, exasperated.

"Well simple," I said with a smile on my face. "We give her the one thing she wants more than anything else in the world.

My wife's face wrinkled in confusion. "Well what is that?"

"We tell her who hurt her and murdered her sister."

***

"Here you go baby," Trevor said handing me a cup of peppermint tea. Ever since I left my parents place I could not seem to get rid of the chills. I was wrapped in a blanket and on my second cup of tea but I was still shivering. It was weird to be sitting here with Trevor listening to him call me baby and yet at the same time it also seemed so natural.

It was like I finally felt at home. I know in my heart that Trevor really is my husband and that I am meant to be with him for the rest of my life. But it doesn't mean that I can erase the past five years of me living as Kevin's wife. I deleted a whole section of my life for five years and now I just want to remember my past and wipe out the past five years. Why do things have to be so complicated? "Tell me what you are thinking," Trevor said turning my head to look at him.

"It's all just so much," I said trying to think of how to explain things to him. "I mean my feelings and half of the things I have been so confused about now make sense. But I still don't know who attacked Chloe and me. I remember calling her now to tell her about Kevin and our father but I still don't even remember her arriving at our house. That day is still a blank. To top it off, who tried to drown in me in the ocean and why would someone want to hurt me again?"

"It's getting late, how about we get some sleep and once we feel refreshed in the morning we can come up with a list of possible suspects and I will check them out. I told my captain I needed some personal time and he told me to take the rest of the week off so I have time to check out anything we come up with," he said in a very factual manner. "Why don't you give me your keys I have a friend on the force that can grab your car in the morning so you will be able to stay here and relax tomorrow or if you want to go to the spa and spend the day relaxing you will be able to do that. One thing is for sure, you will not have to worry about anyone hurting you again because that will not happen."

"You won't have to check them out alone. We have been figuring this out together and we will continue to do that."

"No," he said firmly in a louder voice. He grabbed my hands and looked into my eyes intensely, "I lost you once and I refuse to put you in any kind of danger again. In fact my number one priority in life is to keep you safe. You have no idea how hard the past five years have been. I spent every day missing you and feeling like I could never love anyone ever again. The truth is, I don't think I could of fallen in love with anyone else because I love you so much that it hurts and I am so thankful that I have been given this second chance with you. I will make sure that it is not screwed up for us again."

I looked into Trevor's wild, intense eyes and felt every part of me falling in love with him yet again. I never felt this way with Kevin even when we were on good terms. The intensity of our love is something I could never explain to anyone. He's my second half and completes me in every way that a husband could. I quickly slid into Trevor's arms and kissed him hard and passionately. We both got lost in the moment as he picked me up and carried me to the bedroom. We slowly made love to each other and everything that had been jumbled up in my head was erased, which only left thoughts of pure love for this man that was my true husband and partner.

***

I sat in the dark, sitting on my couch drinking a glass of red wine. I needed to unwind before I went to bed. I feel like I have been living in a blur for the past five years. My nights have been filled with nightmares and my days have been filled with knots in my stomach and bad migraines. Nothing happened like it was supposed to. How can fights turn so quickly and things get so out of control. Most people would probably describe me as an evil person. They may be right. I don't feel evil though, I did what I did at the time with the best of intentions. Everything just went so horribly wrong. One thing is for sure, when I go to bed tonight I know that I will have the same nightmare that I have every other night: the shocked look of horror in Chloe's eyes as she crumpled over when I shot her. I also know I will wake up in the morning with the same thought going through my head. Breanna is the one that is supposed to be buried in the ground, not Chloe.

Chapter 16

I woke up slowly and turned to take hold of Breanna. My eyes popped open when I realized she wasn't there. I sat up with a jolt and scanned my eyes over the room. "Breanna, baby where are you?"

"Right here," she said in her angelic voice. She walked in the room carrying two cups of coffee wearing nothing but my t-shirt. I felt my eyes crinkle in a smile. She used to always wear my shirts in the morning before she would get dressed for the day. I used to joke what was the point of us ever getting her pajamas when she would never wear them. She was happiest wearing something that I had already worn. "I thought we could use some caffeine to start our day out right," she set down the coffee cups and sat down next to me in the bed twirling her hair around her finger. She seemed almost nervous and unsure of herself. "If we are going to work together to form a list, and you are heading out to figure out the final part of this mystery then we need a cup of my magical coffee to help us get going. Plus I really need to figure out my next chapter." She took a shaky breath and looked up at me with her big worried eyes.

"Your next chapter?" My voice when up an octave alarmed at what she was insinuating. "Baby, our next chapter is being together. Restarting our lives where we left them. We missed so much time together I don't want to miss another moment."

She grabbed my hands in hers, "Now that I remember I can't imagine not being with you too, but Trav my head is spinning here. I just remembered who I am and even though I remember it doesn't just erase the past five years. I know our plan was to have a life in Boston and maybe that is still the best plan with everything that has happened, but I did have somewhat of a life in Cape Cod even if it wasn't real."

"We don't have to decide anything today, I get it you need time. When you are ready to make a decision we can go wherever you want. If you want to stay in Boston that's what we'll do, if you want to go to Cape Cod we can do that too. Fuck it we can move to fuckin' St. Thomas if you want. I don't care as long as I'm with you," I said rubbing my thumb across her cheek as I painfully watched a single tear escape from her eyes. "Please don't cry baby we will work this out."

She smiled, "You just made me remember that I love St. Thomas."

"You went there when you were eight. You said it had the bluest water you had ever seen. It was a great trip for you."

She took a shaky breath. "Thank you. I think I just need to take this one step at a time." She looked around the room and crinkled her nose in disgust. "I know that this is where I don't want to live." I let out a hard laugh amused at her distaste in my apartment. "But back to taking it one step at a time. Coffee," she said handing me my cup. "Best part of the day and then playing detectives."

I smiled, "coffee is always a good part of the day, but having you here next to me is even a better start to my day."

I started laughing again, "What!" she said setting the coffees down on the nightstand finally letting a smile onto her face and planting a kiss on my lips and then leaning her body into mine to rest her head on my chest.

"Well," I said holding her tight to me. "One, I am not playing detective I'm actually a detective and two I knew you would hate this apartment. Every time I walked into the front door the first thought in my head was, Breanna would never live here, she would say it is way too masculine and not personal at all."

Her forehead crinkled as she glanced around the room. "It really isn't personal at all, I feel like I walked into a bachelor pad."

I kissed her slowly and passionately until she stopped me. "We can second honeymoon later," she said pushing herself off of me and handing me my cup of coffee, "now we need to write the list of people that would have had a reason to try to kill me and my sister."

"Fair enough," I said letting out a deep frustrated sigh. I just got my wife back, the last thing I wanted to do at this exact second was write lists of people. But, as usual, I knew she was right and everything else in our life would have to wait until we could figure out what someone would gain by hurting her "Alright, well there is the obvious, Kevin. If you had told Chloe what happened then his whole marriage would have been destroyed and everyone would know what a creep he truly is. And let's also not forget about your father. We know he was on the scene, since he is the one that found you, and we know that he would not want you to tell Chloe that he was more interested in having Kevin as a son in law than both of your safety. Let's also not forget that he did choose to switch your identity to make you Chloe, if your father would do that who knows what else he would do? If either of them caused the accident, though, we are still in the dark as to who tried to drown you yesterday. They both have solid alibis. My final thought is, of course, your ex-best friend Annabelle. She has made it perfectly clear how much she hates you."

I looked over at Breanna realizing she was being quiet and saw a tear trickle down her cheek, "Baby!" I said, panicked. I didn't mean to upset her. And I had to kick myself. She wasn't one of the other detectives. I couldn't talk to her like I could talk to my partner on the force. She has always been sensitive and she has been through so much in the past 48 hours.

"At one point in time each of these three people was the most important person in my life. Now there is a reason that each of them could have wanted to hurt me. How can someone go from being your all to being your worst enemy?"

"I know honey, this isn't easy. But you left Cape Cod for a reason, you realized that you didn't want to sink to their level. You are such a wonderful, caring person; it isn't you, its them. You have to remember that they didn't do what they did because they hate you, well, maybe Annabelle did, they have always done everything thinking of only themselves." I kissed her hands and wiped the tear off her face. I saw the pain she was feeling as her world was being ripped apart. I just wished that there was more I could do to shield her.

"I know," she said, clearing her throat apparently trying to pull herself together. "I know you are right, we are going to figure all of this out and then I am going to put all of these people behind me and us."

"I think that sounds perfect," I said sliding out of bed. I gave her a quick kiss, "Now time to shower and get back to being a detective. The sooner we can find answers the sooner we can leave Boston and give you a vacation away from all of this." I walked away from her heading to the shower, and while I had made my voice as optimistic as possible, the truth was I was so scared I would not be able to find the truth. More important than that, I was terrified I would not be able to protect her and this time it would not be a mistake that she was murdered.

***

Trevor hurried out the door. I wanted to go with him so badly but he convinced me that it was for the best for me to stay here while he went searching for answers. Before I got to work I figured I should give Lily a call before she thought I was ignoring her.

The phone rang only once this time, "Seriously Chloe, where the hell have you been!"

"I am sorry Lil, but a lot has happened."

"Are you ok? What happened? Tell me everything?"

"I'm ok and I'm not ok. I don't know how to tell you this so I am just going to start from the beginning and tell you everything."

I went through and told her everything from the dreams, to Kevin attacking me to the truth of who I am. Lily said nothing but occasionally made gasping noises.

"Well Lil, what do you think? Say something!"

"Chl, I mean… crap, I don't even know what to call you. This is crazy and is so awful. What the crap! I mean seriously… hell... damn… shit! I don't even know how to grasp my head around everything." She took a deep breath like she was trying to gather her thoughts and pull herself together. "I think you have only one option. You may not want to hear this but I am your best friend and you need someone to tell you the truth. Go to counseling with Kevin. I know it seems horrendous to forgive him but what choice do you have? You and Kevin have a good life together, you aren't meant to be the wife of a cop and lets face it, you love your home, you would hate living in Boston. The traffic drives you nuts!"

I had to laugh at that. "Lily you don't get it, I'm not Chloe I'm Breanna, Trevor's my husband and I love him. I just forgot how much. Kevin's a horrible man and I want nothing to do with him. He not only disgusts me but to be completely honest I'm scared of him too. Lil, he hurt me, not once but twice. The only thing you're right about is that yes I do adore Cape Cod. I will figure that out in time though. I haven't had time to process everything but I guess for the moment Boston will be my home and eventually we can move to somewhere with less traffic". I added a bit more sarcastically then I intended. I had to stop and take a deep breath while I remembered I was talking to my best friend who only had one goal and that goal is to help me. "It will be ok," I finished, mostly to convince myself.

"Take time to think things over Chloe, I think you will come to a different conclusion," Lily said firmly with no emotion in her voice, clearly in shock. "Listen I have to go, I have a ton of things to do today, but pull it together and

Don and I will see you and Kevin at dinner next Thursday. Bye, love you!" she said in a strained fake happy voice as she slammed the phone down before I could respond.

She was clearly in shock over what I had told her. I felt myself getting angry but then I had to remind myself how confusing this must be for her. She just found out that the best friend she grew up with is dead and her new best friend is someone completely different and is leaving town. If that doesn't make it bad enough, her husband's full career rides on Kevin's career, who is a psychopath, about to lose everything. This is going to affect her life dramatically. I just needed to let her soak all of the information in.

I had to push thoughts of Lily to the side, though. It was time to focus. I sat down to do some brainstorming of my own. I was so furious with my father, Kevin and even Annabelle but I still wanted to believe that they wouldn't have murdered Chloe. There had to be someone else, in fact, maybe it was someone we didn't know. For all we knew it could have just been an intruder coming in to rob us and Chloe and I surprised him by being there. I knew that was extremely unlikely but I really wanted to believe that no one I knew could have committed this heinous crime.

A part of me wanted to sit down with Annabelle again, and this time it wouldn't be clueless Chloe sitting down with Annabelle but it would be me, her old best friend and the girl who has been dead for five years, Breanna. I still can't recall everything but at least I remember who I am and a lot about my and Annabelle's history. I knew Trevor wouldn't be crazy about it but I ignored that and picked up my phone and dialed a number that surprisingly came back by memory. It was strange, I could recollect these little things and I could still not dredge up a lot of the big memories.

Annabelle answered after just two rings, "Hello, this is Annabelle Dawson how can I assist you," she answered in a breathy voice. I had to roll my eyes; Annabelle has tried to use sex appeal to get whatever she wanted from the second she started to develop breasts. I remembered when we were in the eighth grade and she wanted to copy Andy Baley's worksheet for history class. She batted her eyes and twirled her hair around her fingers and told him how handsome she thought he was and she would be so grateful to him if he would do this favor for her just once. For the rest of the year she copied his papers and she had perfect scores on all her history worksheets without doing any work, classic Annabelle.

"Hi Bell," I said remembering when we were young and first saw Beauty and the Beast. I loved the name Bell and told Annabelle that we could call her Bell from now on and it would be just like she was a princess.

Annabelle said nothing but I could hear her sharp intake of breath. "Bell are you there?"

"Bre?" she said in a soft hushed tone.

"Yes it's me, I know this is confusing but if we can meet I can try to explain everything to you.

We sat on the phone for a second in silence and then I heard something that I could hardly believe. Annabelle started crying. I have only seen her cry maybe two other times and those were the day her beloved bunny, Sam, passed away and the day her first boyfriend broke her heart.

As she cried my heart momentary reached out to her. How had we gotten here? We had been friends our whole lives. How are we now enemies? How is it possible that I'm now in the position that I'm trying to figure out if she murdered my sister? The sympathy quickly turned to resentment as the flashes of her laughing while I was raped went through my head. No matter what happened in my life from now on that is something I could not get over. I know that it was many years ago and I should search for forgiveness, but she sat there and watched and laughed as my whole world got torn apart by the man that said he loved my sister. The man who for the past five years said he loved me as well.

"Bre, I can't believe you are alive," she said in a distant voice.

"Annabelle, please, I need to meet with you and talk with you about everything. I think that you owe me at least that after everything you did to me."

She stopped crying into the phone and everything got silent for a minute. "Bell are you still there?" I asked in confusion.

"After everything I did to you?" she said in a low trembling voice. The anger that she was exuding mimicked all of the anger I felt towards her. "This town hates me still to this day because of you. My senior year of high school was miserable because of you. I couldn't go to my dream college and my life became shit. Instead of standing by me and being my friend you treated me like a piece of garbage just like everyone else at the school did."

"You watched me get raped," I said in between the angry tears that started to go down my face.

I could tell now that she hadn't stopped crying either and in an awful screaming voice she started to yell back at me. "Boo hoo you had sex with the hottest man in Cape Cod. Most people would have dreamed of that happening to them and instead you are acting like we destroyed your life. We did you a favor."

"I was mistaken, I have no need to see you in person. I'm sorry you got caught cheating and even more sorry that you think what happened to you in high school compares to what you watched happed to me and then laughed about. You were always my best friend, but while you think I should be thankful for what happened, you should know that until my sister was murdered that was the single worst day of my life and I had nightmares about that incident every night until I lost my memory." I quickly slammed the phone down on the nightstand after hitting end on my cell.

I started to cry uncontrollably again. I didn't think I had any more tears in me and I was pretty sure the puffy eyes I had been wearing the last few days were never going to go away. I cried for my and Bell's past friendship as good memories floated through my head and for the horrible person she had turned out to be. How could my sweet, devoted best friend turn into such a horrible monster that gets off on hurting people? I also cried for whatever the perceived role I might have played leading to her becoming this way. Maybe if I had been slightly more understanding when she was going through a hard time in high school things would have turned out differently. Finally, as I calmed down and my sobs turned into light hiccups something occurred to me: the past was an awful thing but at least it brought me to Trevor and that was a relationship I now had to protect. It was already taken from me once and there was only one way to prevent that from happening again and that was to figure out what had happened.

The piercing sound of my cell phone ringing took me out of my thoughts.

"Hello," I said without even bothering to glance at who it was on the other end.

"Bre, thank god you answered!" bellowed my father into the phone. I sighed and rolled my eyes and starting to put down my phone and hang up without responding. "Bre, before you hang up please wait, I need to meet with you! I need to tell you who murdered your sister."

***

"Miss Dawson, your 3:00 is still sitting out here in the waiting room," said my receptionist through the intercom on my phone.

I picked up my phone and dialed her extension. "Cheri, I am going to need you to cancel my 3:00 along with the rest of my appointments for the day. Tell them that I have a family emergency and for his inconvenience today his next appointment will be free.

"Of course, Miss Dawson, is everything ok? Anything I can help with?"

"No thank you, Cheri. After cancelling out my afternoon please feel free to take the rest of the afternoon off." I quickly hung up the phone and took a few deep breaths. It had taken all my strength to keep my voice from shaking as I spoke into the phone. I could not remember the last time I felt so rattled. I know that I have done some pretty horrible stuff in my past, and present for that matter, but I always felt justified in everything that I had done. People had wronged me and I always believed an eye for an eye. For the first time in my life I had lost the happiness that causing Chloe and Breanna's pain and suffering had given me. I never thought I would have to face or talk to Bre again and that blast from the past felt earth shattering. I put my head in my arms and started crying saying to myself, "Oh Annabelle, what have you done, what have you done?"

***

I kept going over the list of people in my head. It could have been a random person, but very unlikely. The police had never suspected a random break in, it was too violent and there was nothing of huge value in the home. Kevin was at the top of my list. I couldn't think of a person who I hated more. He is such a despicable human being and I know he is capable of anything. He already committed rape twice that I know of, who is to say he would not commit murder. It was taking everything in me not to rush over to his house at that very moment just so I could pummel him.

I took a deep breath and unclenched my hands, trying to get myself to calm down. Getting all worked up right now wasn't going to do anyone any good. I knew logically it made sense to call the Captain and tell him what was going on. The news that Breanna is alive and Chloe is dead could change the whole case. Although, at the end of the day it's still very possible that Breanna was the main target. While the judge was definitely a piece of work and just the thought of him made me furious, I had my doubts about him being evil enough to do this. While he certainly committed his share of crimes and wrongdoings he was motivated by greed and selfishness and he would have nothing to gain by hurting either of the girls. Chloe was his little princess and Breanna never talked about what a scumbag he was, instead she was hidden away from the public and prying eyes of Cape Cod. I didn't want to rule out anything though, there was still a possibility that he knew that Breanna was about to tell Chloe everything and he could have followed Chloe to try to talk sense into both of them. Things could have turned ugly and somehow gone horribly wrong. Then, in fear, he could have lit the house on fire to hide what he had done.

The sad thing is there are multiple possibilities. The final possibility that makes sense is Annabelle. She holds so much anger and hate for both of the sisters. Who knows what she is capable of. The only reason I am not convinced that it could have been Annabelle is out of everyone, she had no reason to come to Boston that day. Breanna had been out of her life for a while and it doesn't seem like Chloe really wanted much to do with her ever.

With that thought in mind it made sense to try to talk to her again. She seemed to have some sort of relationship with Kevin and maybe he had confided in her at one point or another. If she is innocent then hopefully she will feel like she has nothing to hide. The biggest thing I have going for me right now is that she doesn't know that I think she is probably innocent and I can try to play with her mind a little. It actually would be nice to mess with her for a little bit, she has certainly messed with Breanna for years.

***

"Kevin, she's coming over. We can make her see our point of view. If everything works out like planned then she will understand and be back at your home by the end of the day," I said almost too joyfully into the phone. I was trying to believe that this would fix all of our problems. But I also had to be realistic, Bre was pissed and hurt, and rightfully so. There was a very good chance that she would never forgive either one of us and I can't say I blame her. I could not sit around and think negatively though. I had to hope that it would all work out and that she would forgive me and realize that she did not want to lose her family.

"Dad that sounds perfect! I will head right over to your house. You are her father and I am her husband. She loves her life and I can't imagine that she will want to just throw that away. I should be there in thirty minutes. I'll see you then."

"Ok, I'll see you soon."

I hung up the phone and could sense someone behind me. "This better work," my wife said in a tense voice.

"Honey it will, stop worrying, I will take care of everything." I bent down to kiss her on the cheek, she turned from me before I could kiss her and walked into the other room. If this didn't work out not only would I lose my daughter but I might also lose my marriage. I couldn't handle that which meant only one thing; this had to work.

***

My heart was pounding, what did my dad mean? Was it even possible that he could know who the murderer is? In my heart I knew that it was probably a trap but it was a risk I had to take. If it wasn't a trap and I didn't go then there was a chance I would never know.

I sat down at the table to collect my thoughts. Should I call Trevor and let him know what I was doing? The answer was yes, probably, but I didn't want to take the chance that he would tell me not to go. I knew going wasn't the smartest decision in the world but I decided to wait to tell him until after I talked to my father. I would leave him a note in case he came home while I was out. While I didn't want him to talk me out of this I also didn't want him to worry. He has been through enough in the past five years and I knew he wanted to protect me. I loved this about him and I had the same obligation to him.

As I hopped into my car, thankful that it arrived after my conversation with my dad, I couldn't help but think, what if my dad was telling the truth. How would he know who did it? Did he just find out or has he known all along? If he has known all along why didn't he turn the person in? I owe it to Chloe to find some answers; at one point in time she was my best friend and the closest person in my life. While we had drifted apart, she is still forever my sister and nothing can change that. My phone rang and I saw it was Trevor. I hit ignore. I just didn't want to be tempted to lie to him. He will see my note when he gets home and he will understand everything.

The traffic on RT 3 was terrible, which was leaving me alone with my thoughts longer than I wanted. Who would my father protect? There were only two people that popped into my head, Kevin and himself. Kevin he has protected multiple times before, but would he really protect him from being punished for murdering one of his own daughters? Then, of course, he would do anything to protect himself. Is he capable of this, though? The thoughts brought new tears to my eyes because I really didn't know. I didn't feel like I even knew him anymore. He let me pretend to be my dead sister for five years. He loved Chloe much more than me and he chose to kill my identity as Breanna off and let her live on. I let more tears stream down my face until they started to blur my vision.

Ok, enough with the tears. I will never get answers if I sit in the corner and cry all day long. I took a deep breath as I final pulled off US 6 and gave myself the pep talk I was in dire need of hearing, hang in there Breanna, you can do this. You are strong and you can do anything you put your mind to.

***

Crap! Why isn't Breanna answering her phone? I felt a tug in my stomach like something wasn't right. Even though it's been 5 years, I knew her better than anyone. With her loss of memory I know her better than she knows herself right now. I was positive that she would be waiting by her phone to hear updates. That is, of course, unless something happened. I was pulling up to Annabelle's office and did not have the time to rush home and get back before the end of the workday. I made a quick decision and picked up my police radio. "This is Detective Cading, are there any officers near Back Bay?"

"Roger, Cading, this is Officer Norman I am near Back Bay."

"I need to you to swing by Garrison Square Apartments and do a welfare check on the woman inside of apartment 3C. Her name is Breanna. Just tell her I sent you."

"Roger that."

I took a deep breath, glad that she was being checked on. Immediately my phone started lighting up with calls and texts from friends of mine on the force confused by the radio call. I brushed them off and told them I would explain later. The only ones I do have to give a real explanation to are my captain and my partner. I decided I should give my captain a call first. I quickly told him what happened.

"Shit Cading. Why am I just hearing all of this now? This case is officially back open and I can assure you its getting top priority. But same as before, stay away, you cannot be on the case!"

"Captain, I understand," I said in a very tense hushed tone. "But with all due respect, after my initial investigation last time and after I was reprimanded I kept out of it and lost my wife for five years. I'm already at Annabelle's office. She knows who I am and I think she will answer more questions if I'm the one asking. I can't just sit on the sidelines this time."

The Captain gave out an exasperated sigh, "Alright Trevor, You can continue to investigate but once we can make an arrest back off. Your involvement could ruin everything in court. You're not the head detective on the case, you understand me?"

"Yes Captain," I said, relieved he gave in some.

"Ok we will start putting together a team here, and Trevor,"

"Yea," I said waiting to be yelled at some for not telling him sooner.

"I'm happy you have Breanna back, I always liked her and have missed her as well," the Captain said in what shocked me as an almost chocked up voice.

"Thank you Captain, I appreciate that." I hung up the phone with a small smile on my face. I do have my Breanna back and what was not to like, she is the most giving gracious, amazing woman I have ever known. I slowly got out of my car to head up to Annabelle's front door wishing that I had heard back from Officer Norman so this nervous ball in my stomach would go away.

***

"Annabelle!" Screeched Cheri into the phone causing me to drop my pen and scare me out of the daydream I was having. I quickly wiped the tears from my face feeling embarrassed for still crying. I am usually so put together, talking to Breanna really rattled me. I started thinking about all of our happy times together as children. Then I couldn't help but wonder what kind of person I really was. I have been filled with hate for so long that I had never stepped back and looked at my own actions. After the fire I just wrote Bre out of my life. The only time I even thought about her was when I saw whom I thought was Chloe. Due to Chloe's charmed life I could only feel glee about my actions. I tried not to start crying again when I couldn't help think again what a rotten person I had become.

"Yes?" I responded in an overly cheery voice trying to cover up the fact that I was a hot mess.

"That Detective is here to see you again. I told him you were not seeing any clients today but he insists that he see you right away and says he is coming into your office regardless."

"Tell him I have nothing to say to him. Anything that he wants to know tell him I have told his wife." I immediately regretted not leaving the second I cancelled my appointments. I could not handle seeing him right now.

I hadn't even known Breanna was married. For the first time I had a thought go through my head that started to cheer me up. If Chloe is really Breanna, does that mean she is back with Trevor? More importantly does that mean Kevin is single? I knew deep down that we were always meant to be together. This man could be my ticket to becoming the Governor's wife.

"Cheri, I changed my mind. Send him in."

"Good thing because he started heading back there the second he heard you mention his wife."

I looked up at my door and was not surprised to see it fly open. "What the hell do you mean, what you said to my wife? What did you say to her?"

"Hello Detective Cading, what a nice surprise. I wasn't expecting to see you again." His face was crimson red with anger and his eyes were narrow with suspicion. I took a second to study him. I could see what Breanna saw in him. He's definitely a very attractive man. He is exactly her type. I remember during one of our slumber parties when we were young we wrote down a list of all the qualities we wanted in our future husbands. Bre pretty much nailed it with her husband. He's exactly what she had said she wanted.

He started to say something but his phone rang. He gave me a quick look and then looked down at who was calling him. "I have to take this," he muttered more to himself then to me. "Hello. What do you mean she isn't there? Where is she? She's going to meet who? Why the hell would she be going to meet her father? I understand. Thank you for calling and letting me know."

He hit end on his phone and slammed his hand down on the desk. So Breanna was going to meet the judge. I had to wonder though, why it was such a mystery that she was going to talk to her dad. I did find it interesting, though, that it clearly upset the detective so much. They had just reunited and they were already having issues.

He sighed heavily and looked up at me, "So, back to you, what were you talking about? What the hell did you say to my wife?"

"Nothing to worry about. We just got into a bit of an argument. But after I had some time to really reflect on everything I realized I should probably apologize to her. I mean this whole thing is pretty crazy after all. The fact that she has been alive all this time and we have all been spending time with her and thinking she was someone else. I can hardly believe it myself," I said flipping my hair over my shoulder feeling a lot better and surer of myself.

"I would appreciate if you didn't talk to her at all," Trevor said with a snarl in his voice. "I also would like you to answer some questions for me, starting with, did you and Kevin go over to my house that day planning on hurting Breanna or did everything that happened just occur in the heat of the moment?"

I almost had to laugh. "Are you seriously coming into my office and accusing me and the Governor of committing crimes. You have to be crazy. Everyone knows that I would never hurt a fly and the Governor; well the whole country knows how great he is and how lucky everyone is to have him in office. Why don't you just go home to your wife and the two of you leave the rest of us alone. The Governor is much better off not having her in his life and I think that everyone would appreciate if the two of you would just disappear."

Trevor gave a little laugh. "If you think that I am just going to ignore the fact that someone attempted to murder my wife and did murder her sister you are crazy. She is going home with me but we will not disappear until we know exactly what happened and until someone is behind bars. So I suggest you start cooperating or everyone is going to think that you have something to hide, and before you know it you will be arrested. Plus don't forget that I know what you did and I should just arrest you right now for that alone!"

My eyes popped open and I felt my stomach tighten up. How did he know? I thought I had gotten away fast enough but he must have seen me. I quickly regained my composure and went on the offensive.

"You know what Detective Cading, maybe I do have something to hide and there is nothing you or anyone else can say to me to get me to tell you. Just because you know about the ocean means nothing. She lived, I didn't hurt anyone. I suggest, though, that you leave Kevin alone or I suspect that your pretty little wife will continue to have problems in her future and maybe next time you won't be around to rescue her!" I said, turning my back to Trevor and grabbing my purse.

I felt my body spun around and thrown up against the wall. All of the air was knocked out of my lungs by the impact and I was shocked to be staring into Trevor's now black eyes that were blazing with fury. "If you were not a woman I would knock you out right now. Understand one thing, if you dare to threaten Breanna again you will not be dealing with me in my official capacity, you will be dealing with me, one extremely pissed off husband who will do anything to protect his wife. Trust me, that is a lot worse than being thrown in jail. You may not want to speak to me now but believe me you will be speaking to me in the future and you will tell me everything you know because you have no idea how nasty I can truly get. I guess none of that matters though, with that confession I can throw you into jail right now."

He stepped back from me to grab his handcuffs from his back pocket. I gave him a quick knee to the groin and it gave me the chance to run out the door and quickly turn around and give him one final look. "Detective you have no idea how truly nasty I can get." I quickly went running out the door not giving him a chance to respond. I ran to my car as fast as I could. I quickly locked my car doors and went fumbling around in my purse. I knew what I had to do. I had avoided doing this for so long but there was no time to wait. I had to do it now. I found what I was searching for and pulled out my cell phone. I quickly dialed the number and waited for the person to answer on the other end. It only took a second for the person to pick up.

***

I was driving lost in thought and my phone rang. I quickly picked up not even looking who was calling.

"Bre, change of plans," said her overly cheery voice.

"What are you talking about? Change of plans of what?" I asked genuinely confused.

"I'm now meeting with you and your father and we decided to change up the location. We're now going to all meet at George's Pizza"

"George's Pizza?" I said with confusion. "Why there, it is shut down for renovations. Remember the pipe burst and it flooded. And why are you meeting with us? What do you have to do with this?"

"Your father thought it would be best if I was there with you while he talked to you. And yes, I remember about the renovations, but we thought it would be best to meet on neutral territory and with it being closed no one will be there to disturb us."

"Why did you talk with my father?" With that I heard my phone make a beeping noise. Before I let her answer my question I continued. "Oh crap my phone is about to die. All right, I think it is strange but if that is where my father said that he is meeting me then I guess I will head there. I really don't understand why you are coming but with my phone being at one percent you can explain it to me there."

"Alright see you there" she said then ending the phone call.

I hung up to my beeping phone. I can't believe I forgot to charge it last night. On top of everything I had forgotten to bring a phone charger. I guess I get a pass on a dead phone since I have had so much going on with my life. I still don't know why she is coming, why she talked to my father and why they switched where we are meeting but I guess everything will make sense when I get the full explanation when we meet. I tried to focus on something, anything other than everything going on in my life right now. I switched my thoughts to unimportant things. It will be interesting to see George's Pizza and see how much the flood hurt the place. Annabelle's uncle is the owner and we spent a lot of time as kids hanging out. We even got to help the cooks and put the toppings on our own pizzas at times. I had to smile. I had a lot of good memories of the place and it was nice that good memories were coming back to me as well.

My phone rang and I saw it was Trevor and decided I could not avoid him any longer. He would have to understand that I have to do this.

"Honey, I love you but why the hell are you going to meet your father without me?"

"I'm sorry Trev, but he has some information he needs to tell me and I need to hear what he has to say. I didn't tell you because I was afraid you would try to talk me out of it and even if he's lying and he knows nothing I will continue wondering if I don't go for myself to find out."

He sighed heavily. I smiled because I know him so well I could see him pacing back and forth in my mind. I hate to worry him but once this is over then we can go off just the two of us and start our lives over again. "Alright Bre, but I'm coming to your parent's house. I'm not going to leave you alone with him after everything he has done to you. Plus you will be pleased to know I found out who tried to drown you but not pleased to know that unfortunately she got away from me."

"Seriously! Tell me everything when you get here but we…." Of course my phone dies before I can get out that we are no longer meeting at the house. Isn't that always how it goes? Phone decides to die at the least convenient time. I sighed heavily. I guess I will just have to borrow one of their phones to let him know where we are headed. I pulled onto Commercial Street ready to hear what they had to say, hopeful that this wasn't just a complete waste of time.

Chapter 17

"Why is she running late?" She is never late!" said the Judge pacing back and forth in the house.

"She will be here Dad, we have to believe that. She probably just got stuck in rush hour traffic. Her phone keeps going to voicemail so it must have died. She always forgets to put a phone charger in her purse so she has no way to charge it. This is actually perfect; this gives us time to go over what we are going to say to her. We need to make sure that she understands that we both love her and have never meant to harm her in any way. You understand that I have a problem and that I'm going to get help; that is why you have stuck by me."

"Yes and I also know that you will never harm her again because you love her. And I didn't do everything because I wanted her to believe she is Chloe or because I favor Chloe over her but because I wanted my daughter close to me; my only surviving daughter who was injured near me. Now that she knows the truth and her memory is coming back she needs us more than ever. We are her support system and as her doctors have told her in the past she needs a strong support system throughout this."

"This all sounds like a bunch of bullshit if you ask me," Trevor's voice said breaking into our conversation.

"Where the hell did you come from," I yelled jumping back. Nothing I hated more than having someone sneak up on me.

"I talked to Breanna and she told me she was coming here to find out who killed her sister and I thought that I should come and hear the confession as well. After all, whoever did this did tore her away from me for five years. Plus I don't trust the two of you around her for a second. The only reason both of you are not in jail yet is because I haven't been able to convince Bre to press charges. But trust me, once everything dies down and we figure out who is responsible then she will press charges and Judge and Governor you both will be sent away for a long time."

"Some threat, Cading," bellowed the Judge. "You and I both know that regardless of what has happened in the past Breanna will never have us arrested. We are her family. You are a blip in her life, a part of her teenage rebellion. She is a grown woman now. Your time with her has passed and now, once things get settled down, she will realize that family is the most important thing to her, it always has been. She will come home to Kevin and you will be just a distant memory."

I couldn't help but smile. That was such a pleasant thought and I hoped to God the Judge was right. The main thing I had learned through this whole ordeal is how much I do love Chloe, and not the real Chloe who died five years ago but the Chloe who is coming to meet me right now. I understand she was born Breanna but she is now Chloe and I love her now and will love her until I die.

The crash of what I knew to be a very expensive vase ripped me out of my thoughts. Trevor's face had turned bright red and he was shaking with rage, so much so I even took a step back. "You arrogant jackass. A blip in her life, are you fucking kidding me? I'm her husband! I am her family. You may biologically always be her father but you lost the right to call yourself a real father when you realized that your other daughter died and you asked a young medical examiner to not even do an autopsy on your daughter and confirm that it was Breanna's body on his slab. You stole five years of her life from her and from me. You didn't act like a father you acted like a selfish prick. Therefore from now on out you are out of our life. You're now not family you're just a memory. Whatever control you think you possess over your family is over. It ended the second your daughter learned who she really is. She walked away from you once before and now she is walking away without looking back. As for Kevin he has never been Breanna's family. He's a fucking rapist who you allowed to pose as her husband for five years. Fucking hell you allowed him to sleep next to her. A rapist, a fucking rapist next to your daughter! What kind of monster are you? You know what, screw this you can make your confessions down at the precinct. Once Breanna is here I am having you both taken in. Where is she? She should be here by now," Trevor finished mumbling to himself looking at the time on his cell phone.

There was no way he could take us to the precinct. Chloe wouldn't press charges against me and we weren't really going to tell her who killed her sister. We just said that to lure her here so we could reason with her. It doesn't matter what this pig thinks. It doesn't matter what anyone thinks. I know I'm not a rapist. Chloe and the Judge both know I'm not a rapist. I may have my faults but having sex with my wife is hardly rape and what happened with Breanna was just some teenage rebellion. I took a deep breath and refused to feel nervous about Trevor's threats. I was beginning to feel nervous about Chloe's tardiness though. "We have been wondering the same thing," I said, feeling a knot form in my stomach. Something didn't feel right. The judge was right, Chloe was never late. I can't imagine that her discovering she is Breanna would all of a sudden change that about her.

"She should be here", Trevor said mostly to himself. "When I talked to her she wasn't far from here and I know that traffic is not bad right now."

The three of us all looked at each other thinking the same thing. Where are you, love? Please be safe.

***

I couldn't help but feel gleeful after I hung up the phone. I put down the mirror and did my usual adjustments to my hair and makeup. My heart was racing. This is what I have been waiting for since Breanna screwed me over in high school.

I gave myself a little pep talk before I started driving. "Be cool Annabelle, this is your time. Your moment, be calm and everything will go as planned."

I smiled to myself as I started to drive towards my destination. This was the happiest I had felt in a long time. I also knew that after I finished what I needed to do my life could finally start. I would finally get everything that I have ever deserved. It was my time to shine, not Chloe, and not Breanna. They will finally be completely out of the picture.

I smiled wickedly as I started the car and headed out of my parking spot.

***

"Where the hell was everyone?" I thought looking down at my watch. I knew I was a little early but this was getting to be ridiculous. Luckily the spare key to George's was still hidden in the same spot so it was no issue getting inside. The flood had not done as much damage as I expected and looking around the place it looked pretty good. I guessed it would be up and running in no time at all. It was hard to focus on George's though my stomach was in knots. There was a chance I was finally about to get all of the answers I have been waiting so long for. I also knew logically that my father could be lying; it was what he does best. Crap, lying is what he does best. He isn't about to tell me anything he is just telling me another one of his lies.

"This is stupid", I said to myself. I went to grab my purse, which I had set down beside me, and head out the door when I heard a car door slam out front. "Finally," I muttered to myself.

With a jingle of the door she walked on in with a big smile on her face. I looked at her and noticed she was alone and all of a sudden something didn't feel right and I got a nervous feeling in the pit of my stomach.

***

"There haven't been any accidents," I said getting off the cell phone. "But my partner and captain know a few cops over here and have them patrolling looking for her car.

Once they find her they will come here and take you both to the station."

"Christ Cading, can you drop all of the crap about me and Kevin and just focus on the fact that my daughter may be missing," said the Judge while running his hands through his hair. His face had paled earlier and he had still not regained color. He also had seemed to age ten years in the past thirty minutes. It seemed he was finally starting to grasp the severity of his and Kevin's situation. He was about to say something more when the sound of a car door slamming interrupted him.

"Thank God," I said running to the door. Kevin beat me to it and threw open the door ready to welcome Breanna into the house.

"Hello boys, what a welcoming committee. You must have all missed me," said Annabelle in her sensual tone.

"What the hell are you doing here," asked Kevin sounding more than a little annoyed.

"Well you don't have to get snarky with me. I just came here to offer a solution to all of your problems."

"Unless you know where Breanna is, then I don't think you can offer a solution to anyone's problems," said the Judge shaking his head and pouring himself a scotch with his shaky hands.

I grabbed her arm a little too tight and got up close to her face. "Do you know where Breanna is at? Last time I saw you, you were threatening her. I swear to God if you have hurt one hair on her head I will make you wish you were never born. The only reason I'm not arresting you this second is because my main focus is to find her. But trust me once she is found you're going to sit with Kevin and the Judge in the back of the cruiser and get what you deserve."

"Kevin, he is hurting me," she said pouting and ignoring everything I had just said to her.

"Well do you know where she is?" Kevin asked in a demanding tone, completely disregarding her cry for help.

"No I have no idea where she is. I swear," she said in a sad, hurt voice still looking right at Kevin.

"Alright," I said letting her go. "Then what the hell were you talking about having a solution to our problems?"

"I was talking to Kevin not to you," she said making her way beside Kevin.

"What do you want, Annabelle, we really don't have time for any of your games right now," Kevin said sounding annoyed and looking down at his watch again, realizing just how late Breanna now was, something we all couldn't forget even with the distraction of Annabelle.

"You can be with me now Kevin."

"What?" he said looking up at her clearly wondering if she was joking or had just lost her mind.

"You're so concerned with making things right with Chloe, or Breanna, or whoever she is, but you don't have to do that anymore. I can be the perfect politician's wife. Trevor and Breanna can leave town and we never have to see them again and I can take her place. I'll make you so happy," she said trying to put her arms around Kevin's neck. If I hadn't been so worried about Breanna it would have been entertaining to watch.

"Are you crazy Annabelle, I love Chloe and I want nothing to do with you. You are simply a piece of white trash that I used as a sidepiece when I needed one. You mean absolutely nothing to me."

"Kevin! Enough." yelled the judge. "Annabelle we do not have time for this right now. We have to find Breanna and make sure she is safe."

"Hear that Kevin," said Annabelle in a low voice. "Breanna not Chloe! Chloe is dead and is never coming back. Breanna has never liked you and will definitely never love you. Not like me! You're throwing away the best chance of happiness you have ever had!" she said with tears starting to stream down her face. She turned and ran out the door as fast as she could.

"Way to go Governor," I said shaking my head.

"Don't look at me that way," he said. "You screamed at her first."

"Your right, but I'm not going to worry about her now." I had to put together a plan. Worrying about putting the Governor and Judge behind bars had to come later. I needed to find Breanna and make sure she is safe. "I think it is time we all split up and start driving around searching for Breanna."

We all grabbed our keys and hurried to our cars. I quickly called patrol to have them pick up Annabelle for attempted murder because I could not deal with that nut case right now. I knew something was wrong, just like I knew five years ago that something wasn't right, the night Breanna got attacked. I wanted to throw up but I knew that out of all the times I needed to be strong this was number one. Breanna needed me and I needed to find her and make sure she is safe. I couldn't lose her again; I just got her back and was going to make sure she came home to me.

***

"Hey Lil, where is everyone else?" I asked as she walked into George's.

"It is a shame they couldn't make it," she said shaking her head.

"Well that is ok, why don't we just head up to my parents house and ask them to meet us there when they are ready." I said grabbing my purse, trying to sound calm.

As I started walking to the door I noticed she had not budged. "No Breanna, I don't think that's a good idea."

I noticed something glimmering in her hand. But my mind could not seem to register what she was holding. I stood there for a moment feeling nothing but shock. There stood my best friend, my rock, the person who has been there for me for the past five years helping me with any problems I had. She was holding a gun and there was a look of pure hate on her face.

"You couldn't just let things be could you? You ruined things once and we recovered and now you want to just throw things away and ruin it again!"

"Lily what are you talking about?" I said my voice shaking.

***

And all of a sudden it happened. I wondered what it was going to feel like when it did and it felt like an avalanche hit my body. Every memory that had been blocked out of my injured mind just came crushing back. I remembered staring at the invitation for Chloe's wedding and just crying. I knew I could not fail my sister. I knew it was time I stepped up and protected her. I could no longer protect her by hiding the truth but instead I had to tell her everything. I called her. I remember my hands were shaking as I hit her number on my cell phone.

"Breanna what's up? I can't really talk right now; I have a huge test and have to figure out who the florist is going to be for the wedding. On top of everything mom and I just got in a gigantic fight. She said the most hateful things to me. I am so angry my hands are shaking. Anyways, are you calling to RSVP, maybe bring that hottie husband of yours you told me about?"

"No Chloe, I'm not." No matter what issues we ever had we always could tell what the other was feeling by the sound of their voice and we always knew when it was important.

"What is it Breanna," Chloe said, her voice completely switching up.

"I need you to come here, I need to tell you some things. I need to tell you why I left and it is terrible and I'm so sorry for that. But you need to know because I love you and want you safe," I said with tears running down my face. "What I have to tell you had to do with Kevin."

"Bre please stop crying. Whatever you need to tell me about Kevin I will listen. Thank you for finally wanting to tell me the truth about why you left. I will be there as soon as possible. I'm leaving now."

"Thank you Chloe, I love you. Know that I have always loved you and have missed you so much since I left."

With that Chloe started crying on the phone, "I love you Bre and I have missed you so much too. We'll figure this out. We'll figure this out together, I'm on my way."

"Oh Chloe, please don't tell Dad you're coming. This needs to be just a twins secret."

Chloe started crying harder. "Bre I have missed you so much, you know I would never break a twins secret. See you soon."

She hung up and I knew she was telling the truth. Since we were little we had a thing – whenever one of us would yell twin secret it meant we could not tell a single soul ever. It was a sacred thing between us that no matter what we went through or what happened we would never break. It felt like I waited days for her to show up. It was by far the longest few hours of my life. I took one look at her when she pulled up and started crying. We both hugged for a while. It was unspoken. We knew we were best friends and we let things come between us that never should have.

We sat down and I was just about to tell her everything when I heard someone coming in the front door.

"Who's here?" Chloe asked tilting her head towards the door.

"I'm not sure," I said getting up and making my way to the door, sure it was Trevor but not sure why he was home from work so early. I had spoken to him earlier and he said it would be a late night for him because of a case he was working on.

We were both shocked when we saw it was Lily walking through the door. "Lily!" I said shocked and annoyed, looking back at Chloe hurt that she had broken our twin secret.

"I swear I didn't tell her," said Chloe. "I have no idea how she knew I was here."

"She is telling the truth Bre, don't be mad at her. I overheard your phone conversation. I was helping her plan the wedding when you called. Bre, I over hear a lot of conversations and I also over heard Kevin one day talking to Don. I know why you left town and I have no idea why you are trying to ruin both Chloe and my life by bringing her into your drama. Do not drag Chloe into your whole mess," she said looking angry but composed. "Let's go home Chloe," she said reaching out for Chloe's hand.

"Lily what are you talking about?" Chloe said angrily. She always did have the temper between the two of us. Bre and I are talking. It is a conversation that is going to take place whether it is now or later. And I cannot believe the nerve of you! You have known why she has left town and you never told me. She's my sister and you know how much I have missed her. She is my best friend and my other half. It is completely selfish of you to keep this information to yourself. And how in the world would anything she tells me about my fiancé affect you! You are way out of bounds and need to leave!

Lily's eyes went completely shocked and hurt. "How could you even say she is your best friend? I am your best friend," she screamed. And she wants to ruin your marriage! If you break up with Kevin then Don will leave me! He's only with me because I am best friends with you! He knows that Kevin will keep him as his campaign manager if it keeps you happy! Can't you see? She isn't your best friend she is trying to ruin our lives!

"Enough Lily! I'm sick of your selfish crap," yelled Chloe in her face. "You were not invited here, it is time for you to leave."

What happened next seemed to happen in slow motion, Chloe pushing Lily to the door. Lily getting around her and lifting her hand out of her pocked to reveal a gun. I could hear her pull the trigger but could not believe it was happening. Chloe jumped in front of me trying to yell at Lily to stop. I couldn't comprehend how it happened but the next thing I knew Chloe was crumpled in front of me. She jumped in front of me to save my life. "Chloe," I screamed. I fell to my knees and tried to cover up her wound to make the blood stop. "No, no, no! Chloe you are going to be ok, I love you! What did you do? No, please you are going to be ok. You have to be ok!"

With that Chloe looked at me and in her last breath said, "I love you sis, please find happiness and start a new family and love them with all of your heart." Then it was not like you see in movies where her eyes closed and she looked peaceful. All of the life seemed to drain from her eyes and I could see her muscles start to shut down. I started crying hysterically and then remembered what happened. I looked up at Lily who looked white as a ghost and shocked. She had dropped the gun and was just staring at Chloe, not believing what had happened.

"You tried to kill me," I said in disbelief. "You murdered my sister."

With that she refocused and looked at me with such hate it was like a punch in the stomach. I knew I was not safe and I got up and started running towards the back door. As I reached the back door I quickly tried to get the lock off the door to run to my safety when I felt something hit me in the back of the head and everything went black.

***

I looked at Lily's face. It was filled with the same hate I saw five years ago. "You killed Chloe trying to kill me." I said feeling the same disbelief I had felt five years prior.

"I'm sorry Bre, I'm sorry for everything. But I did everything to protect my marriage. Chloe was not supposed to die, you were supposed to die," she said with the gun shaking at me. "I am sorry Breanna, but thank God Kevin still confides in Don and he knew that you were planning on meeting up with your father and Kevin, although I know you thought you were just meeting your father. Now, the time has come that I need you to lose your memory again. I need you to become Chloe again. It's the only chance for my marriage and my happiness. I cannot lose Chloe as my best friend and I cannot lose Don. Everything depends on this. No worries, though, I studied this. As long as I hit you in the right place the bullet won't kill you, you'll just lose your memories again," she said softly, sounding like a completely different person. Sounding so crazy I couldn't even believe it.

I closed my eyes waiting for the gunshot. I had finally gotten all the answers I had been searching for and they were uglier than I could possibly imagine. The gunshot never happened though. I waited and finally opened my eyes to see Lily staring, her wide eyes focused on something behind me. I turned around not sure what to expect and saw my father standing there staring at Lily as if she was the craziest person he had every seen.

"What you are doing," he asked in disbelief. "My God what are you doing?"

***

I was speeding with tears streaming down my face. How could he treat me like that? I've been in love with Kevin for most of my life. How could he just reject me like that? I threw away my friendship with Breanna because of my love for him. I even attempted to kill her. That day she was just in the wrong place at the wrong time. I went out for a walk on the beach and I saw her. My wetsuit was in my car and I threw it on without thinking. I tried to drown her so I could have Kevin all to myself. I have wanted nothing more in life than to be with him. I would have died for him. Now he just threw me aside, treated me worse than all of those awful women treated me. I am not some white trash whore. I'm a person and I deserve to be treated like one. I started speeding faster and faster, flying down the road. I could hear police sirens coming for me and I knew that Trevor had called them and they were looking for me. Then, as if in a dream I could not believe what I saw up ahead. There sat Kevin in his fancy SUV stopped at a traffic light. Before I had time to think about what I was doing I went as fast as I could in his direction. I saw the panic in his eyes when he saw me coming at him and I could tell he knew there was nothing he could do. I smiled right before we collided and thought, if he doesn't want me he won't have anyone else. Then I heard the deafening crash and everything went dark.

***

Where could she be? It doesn't make sense, I thought, as I drove my car around searching for her. If anything happened to her I don't think I could handle it. I barely kept myself together last time and there was no way I could manage to keep it together if I had to go through that again. We are meant to be together and we deserve the opportunity to have a life and a family together. We deserve to be happy.

My radio started going crazy. "This is Detective Cading," I said into the radio.

"Detective we have found your wife's car in front of George's Pizza, do you want us to go in or wait for you?"

"Go in, I will meet you there," I said into the radio, feeling a huge wave of relief as well as panic and confusion. Why the hell was just there? Thank God she is found, but is she is ok inside? I started doing something I hadn't done in a long time. I started praying. I quickly turned on my police lights and hurried in her direction.

***

I stood there in complete shock. There stood my daughter and there stood her best friend but nothing made sense. Lily was holding a gun pointed at her. They grew up together. Seems that no one is who they appear to be. Immediately I knew what I had to do. I had to do anything I could to save my daughter. To make up for all of the terrible things I had done to her.

"I have to," she said looking at me in the eyes. "Don't be mad judge, I won't kill her, I will just turn her back into Chloe. It's what we all want, you said so yourself."

***

I stood there waiting for Lily to shoot me as my dad tried to talk her out of it. It was like I was watching a movie. This could not be my life. But it was and I watched Lily lift up her arm at me and close her eyes as she pulled the trigger, and just like five years ago I closed my eyes and waited for the impact, but just like five years ago nothing happened. I looked down to see my father covered in blood in front of me. Despite everything he did to me he did still love me. He jumped in front of a bullet for me. I dropped to my knees again like I was reliving everything.

"Daddy," I said with tears streaming down my face.

"It's ok princess, I love you. I'm sorry for everything," he said gasping holding his chest, which seemed to be flowing blood. "I have always loved you," he continued with clenched teeth. I didn't want to turn you into Chloe; I just wanted to keep you close. I was selfish and I will always regret the mistakes I have made. I looked at his wound and quickly took off my scarf that was tied around my neck. I tried to cover up the wound but it didn't seem to be helping a ton. She got him right in the chest. This couldn't be happening again. I looked up at Lily with tears streaming down my face. I didn't see hate this time. I just saw nothing. Her eyes looked completely dead, void of all emotion. I could not believe she was the same person that I had spent so much time with for the last five years. She may be an evil human being but at least I know my father loves me. He had to pull through. I should get up and be prepared to run from Lily like I had five years earlier but I couldn't leave my father dying on the floor all alone. Luckily I didn't have to worry about my safety much longer. Police began busting through the doors.

The next hour seemed like a blur. I watched Lily get taken out in handcuffs and put in the back of a squad car as reporters snapped hundreds of pictures. My father was taken out on a stretcher and put in the back of an ambulance. It didn't look like he was going to make it and I would have to deal with the loss of yet another family member. I would have felt so alone but right after the police had busted in another face came running across the lawn with a look of absolute terror in his eyes. I ran as fast as I could at him. Once he saw me relief flooded his face and I jumped straight into his arms,

"Please, please never let me go," I said feeling so safe and calm for the first time in days.

"Never baby, never. You will never be alone again."

"I remembered everything," I said with tears in my eyes. I know who I am and everything that has happened. I have an identity again, even if it's an ugly one. My identity is the daughter of a father who tried to make her into her sister. I'm a girl who everyone wished was dead and her sister alive. It isn't pretty but at least I know who I am," I said in a hushed voice with my head against his chest still holding onto him.

He turned my head to look into his eyes. "You do have an identity. You will always have an identity. You are Mrs. Trevor Cading, the wife of a man who loves you more than anything in the world and a girl who's family loves her so much they would jump in front of a bullet to save her life."

Epilogue

"Honey, hurry up!" I yelled. I couldn't believe it was time. The contractions were happening every four minutes, which according to our Lamaze class meant it was show time. I just knew this baby would pop out any second. Trevor came running out of the bedroom like a deer in headlights with our overnight bag and everything he thought our baby would need after entering the world. I was pretty sure our baby didn't need ten different outfits but hey, this was my first baby as well so who knew. Trevor didn't think the baby needed all of the stuffed animals but I wanted the baby to come into the world knowing that anything she wanted she could have, including two parent's who loved her more than anything.

I laughed when he turned the police lights on his car to zoom us to the hospital. He so abused that light. Almost a year ago I saw his squad car zooming down the road, lights blazing, and I was terrified he was rushing himself into a dangerous situation to later find out he had been hurrying so that he and his partner did not miss the end of McDonald's breakfast. This was one time I was happy about it, though, because the contractions were getting closer together.

So much had happened in the last year since Lily was arrested. Lily would never see the light of day again. I spoke at her trial and asked for her to not get the death penalty. I just didn't see how killing one more person would bring my sister or my father back or bring any happiness to our family. Speaking at her trial also gave me some closure. I was able to tell her that I forgive her, and that while I was going to move on with my life I hope she spent hers thinking about the people she took from this world. Everyone was shocked when I gave her my forgiveness but I didn't do it for her. I did it for myself. I couldn't live in a world filled with hate. It was a huge weight off my shoulders once I decided to get rid of the anger.

I never pressed charges against Kevin. He was left crippled after the car accident and once everything came out, was impeached from office. I spoke with an attorney once and he told me that I was unable to press charges for the earlier rape due to statue of limitations but could press charges for the recent rape. It would be a hard case though. With my earlier memory loss and Kevin's ability to charm a room full of people there was a huge chance that he would be found innocent. I decided I didn't want to precede any further. He would no longer be able to hurt anyone due to the car crash. Plus it gave me peace knowing that know he could live his days knowing that his torn apart life was his own fault and he could suffer all alone.

My mother and I had started spending more time together. She was in therapy dealing with the loss of my father as well as everything he did. Therapy is also helping her deal with the guilt of saying horrible things to Chloe right before she died. I don't know all of the details of the fight but do know that it has been a horrible weight on her conscious for all of these years. We now meet once a week for lunch and she comes to dinner at Trevor and my house on Cape Cod once a week. It's important to her that she gets to know her son in law and they have grown to love each other.

We moved to Cape Cod when I discovered I was pregnant. While I remember my past I couldn't completely erase the past five years of my life. I had fallen back in love with the cape and found comfort there. I also felt it would be a good place to raise a child. Trevor had no problem with the move. He was sad saying bye to his precinct but he was able to get a job as captain at his new precinct with a considerable raise. We found an adorable house perfect to raise a child in and not too far from my mother. We were ready to rebuild our lives there.

Annabelle slowly recovered from the accident and was then taken into custody. She lives with the horror of what she did to Kevin while living in a small cell. She received ten years for the attempted murder of me and an additional ten years for the attempted murder of Kevin. She has spent many days calling and trying to apologize to me for all of the horror she inflicted on me. I am sure she has also tried to call Kevin but I doubt he has taken her calls. I have given her my forgiveness to help my healing process but made sure she knew that while I forgave her for everything I will never forget what has happened either. She knows that she will never be a part of my life.

We arrived at the hospital in record time and I was quickly brought up to a room. The doctors told me that it would not be much longer and it was too late to give me an epidural, which was fine with me because I wanted to have Trevor and my baby as naturally as possible.

After forty-five of the most painful minutes of my life I finally pushed. Then it happened. I heard the most beautiful sound I have ever heard, the sound of a baby crying, my baby crying. Trevor and I considered waiting to know the sex of our child until after she was born but we both had enough surprises to last us a lifetime. I squeezed Trevor's hand and I looked into his eyes. "Please tell me, is she healthy?" I pleaded.

He just smiled and looked at the doctor who was handing me our baby. "Mr. and Mrs. Cading, it is my honor to introduce you to your perfect and healthy baby girl."

"We did it! We created her. She is as beautiful as you are," Trevor said with tears in his eyes. "What would you like to name her," Trevor asked in a choked up voice as he held her tiny hand.

I smiled and looked down at our perfect miracle. "Chloe".

Printed in the United States
By Bookmasters